Hide the Elephant

A Smallish Novel of Largish Proportions

by

Jonathan Dunne

Copyright © 2015 Jonathan Dunne
All Rights Reserved.
No part of this work may be stored, transmitted, or
reproduced in any form without the express written
permission of the author.

This is a work of fiction. Some locations exist while others
don't. Actual locations that do exist have been altered by
the author for the purposes of fiction and not to be
construed as anything other than fiction. Any similarities
that exist between locations, locales of any description real
or fictional including their time-frames and happenings, are
purely coincidental as are any similarities that exist
between persons, dead or alive, including the living-dead.

Dedication:

To the memory of Tommy, our good-hearted, crazy St. Bernard. He brought lots of warm smiles and friendly screams to the household.

RIP
22nd June, 2015

Acknowledgments:

I'd like to thank the following who helped in the writing of this novel:

Ruth, Spain

Sarah, Ireland

Kim, Australia

Lina, Greece

Rebecca, Canada

Ciorstaidh, Scotland

Liselott, UK

Susan, USA

Heather, USA

Lolly, USA

Prologue of Sorts

I wasn't sure how to start this story/diary/account/tour guide/*How to Hide Your Elephant for Dummies*, but I always knew that it would be about me and You-Know-Who – the elephant in the room, so to speak. My old man always told me never do anything during the day that will keep me awake at night, so I'm going to tell you the whole truth and nothing but the truth, so help me God.

I'm writing my whateveryacallit, in this middle-of-nowhere hay-barn with a flock of bleating sheep staring at me with their oblong irises. I am writing because in a few months time, I probably won't be able to remember, or so the doctors tell me. As The Pixies' song goes: *Where is my Mind?* I don't know where it is – I can't remember so you'll excuse me if there are gaping holes in this account – black holes of lost time. Funny how it was my forgetfulness that got me into all of this in the first place. Forgetfulness is one thing, but forgetfulness caused by an illness is something very different.

But Reader, if ever an illness could bring so much joy to my life, then it is here, right now. I'm *awake* for the first time in my life. Did I ever think that I would find myself coming out of retirement (*forced* retirement, I add with a sprinkle of sour grapes) *in* my retirement?

I *see* for the first time in my life, Reader!

And for the readers among you who think illness is no laughing matter, then you're right, but you're also wrong. It *is* a laughing matter if I *say* it is, right *now*, listening to the sheet-rain pelting the roof of this old barn that we're holding up in as fugitives, my elephant and I, being stared at by suspicious sheep with a hunger on me to beat the band.

What has brought me here, you ask? The answer is simple: I only want to spend some quality bonding-time

1

time with my elephant, Sinbad, for reasons you will soon understand. And while I'm at it, maybe these special days and nights will give me something to remember when the rest blows away in the wind.

Try explaining that to the judge, right?

"So, let me get this right," the man in the comical, curly wig would say, "'you kidnapped – *stole* – an elephant from the zoo and rode him cross-country at night for some *bonding time?* Could you not have just given him a treat?'"

I admit that it is hard to understand if you're not me, so step into my shoes for the next few pages, Reader. C'mon, don't be shy – they're not smelly, though I make no promises as I've already been on-the-run two or three days, can't remember.

Speaking of being on-the-run, it's only a matter of time before the law catches up with me…

Oh, mercy!

My Miniature Life

My name is Mick Munroe, but you can call me Mick Munroe. I live in an empty brown-brick, terraced, ghost house just outside Phoenix Park in Dublin. My house is full of Post-Its of various hues and colours, which remind me of dates, times, events, that kind of thing. If you're looking for the fridge, just check under the Post-Its. Why? I'm getting to it.

Can you see my house, Reader? Are you looking at it on a sunny day or is it raining in your mind's eye? Is my place wedged in between other identical houses or is it a gable-ender? What number do I live at? I'll let you decide. I'll give you a clue: walk along my street. If you listen hard enough, you just might hear me playing my harmonica. It used to belong to my old man. He handed it down to me in his will (that was about all) and there were no hygiene health warnings in those days, no sir.

My ghost house is a few minutes car-ride from Dublin Zoo.

I've been working at the zoo as a keeper for forty-two years and my father, God rest his weary soul, for another four decades before me. And *his* father before him…we go all the way back to the Victorians and the grand Dublin Zoo opening on September 1st, 1831, if my memory serves me correctly – but *don't* trust my memory, Reader. My family has got the zoo in our blood, so to speak, "a touch of the exotic" as my Gloria – my Glow – used to say. Something *very* special connects my deceased old man and me and it's not just the zoo, but I will get to that in just a minute. And it's *not* the harmonica…

Reader, Gloria (Glow to you and me because she was my Glow) passed away two years ago, but it seems like yesterday: cancer – I don't need to say anymore, do I? We all know it's a dead-end street when one poor, lost soul takes the wrong alleyway. I hope, in the near future, a reader is reading this whateveryacallit and is amazed at the times I live in when there is no cure for the Big C, as I do now, reading about tuberculosis.

Sorry, I'm rambling. Reader, give me a dig in the ribs when I do this…

This is why I call it my ghost house – because it's full of the ghosts of memories. It's not haunted or anything like that.

We promised that we'd go on loving each other in death. We vowed to each other that the opening and closing hours of the local cemetery *wouldn't* separate us. Why should it? We vowed to each other that we wouldn't bow to the system and be buried in a communal graveyard with a bunch of dead strangers – it's bad enough having to live with strangers in an Old Folks Home besides taking the next step and being *buried* next to them. Don't get me wrong, Reader, I've got nothing against strangers, dead or alive, but the haunting prospect that Glow and I would not be together forever *always* scared us. We didn't go around the house contemplating the macabre subject of death, mulling it over as we did the washing-up, but we *did* mention it once or twice as every subject eventually surfaces in a life-time marriage. I never wanted to share my Glow with *anybody*. I just hoped that I wouldn't be around to see it. But I am…

You see, we promised that we'd bury each other in the backyard of our brown-brick terraced house.

Morbid? Reader, unless you've ever been married to a terminal husband or wife or long-term girlfriend or boyfriend, you'll never know the late-night conversations and the desperation that helps come to terms with non-existent prospects. Many times, we spoke of the most macabre subjects in a funny way to help us deal with something that was *nightmarish*. The only time we stopped having nightmares was while we slept.

Whoever went first would go in the back-yard, under the shade of the apple tree. That was the deal. And there Glow or I would be happy in knowing that we were still together and not kept apart by a cemetery timetable. *And* we would be reincarnated as a Granny Smith. There's almost something Adam-'n-Eve about it. What could be better?

But our plan hadn't reached as far as the one who would go down second – me. Who buries *me* in our back-yard, under the apple tree? In our collective eye, we imagined a kind of Romeo and Juliet finale, but somebody's got to bury the dead couple. We've got no kids – we almost had one, but *almost* never won the race. Gloria was a superstitious lady and refused outright when I suggested 'artificial means'. Gloria's take on it was that if Mother Nature didn't mean for us to have young ones then it was best not to mess about with the mother of all mothers.

Finally, I buried Gloria in the local cemetery. She wouldn't agree to a crematorium (when she was alive, that is). She always said that was "very final", hmm.

What has this got to do with hiding an elephant, you're asking? I'm trying to get across (in every sense of the word) the hole in my life since Gloria – my Glow – passed on and the drastic decisions we sometimes make in somebody's absence.

Now that the dust has settled, people ask (Glow never let the dust settle and if she saw the layer of dust coating our furniture now she'd…) what I do to "keep busy?" People always stress the urgency that I should "keep busy" now that I'm alone.

Time doesn't exist anymore at my place. It's the 12th February, 2015, but it could be the 30th February at my place. See what I'm getting at? I'm at my most vulnerable when I get home to an empty house. I've been trying to set a routine for myself or "keep busy". Routine structures my evenings and days off; it gives me purpose. If that means "keeping busy" then so be it. I've adapted our house to be more inhabitable – lots of clocks. I love the tick-tock of an old clock and it kind of makes the place sound busy and gives it life, if you have enough of them. In the back of my mind, they are also counting me down… Something else that I've sort of lapsed into recently is looking at live images through webcams of the cities where Gloria and I had planned to go but never got to: Edinburgh and Copenhagen for starters. I'm planning to visit both. Looking at busy city streets from hundreds of miles away keeps the dream alive *and* it also tells me that life never stops, so best jump on-board and enjoy the ride while you can. Another little thing I've resorted to (which I never would've dreamt of if Glow had been in the house) is that I've constantly got the radio on to fill the void, especially at night. Oh, and the lights. How can I forget the lights? They *have* to be on at night; darkness is a lonely place to be on your own. I play my harmonica now and again. I have also taken up the noble art of miniatures. Yep, I collect miniatures. I *have* to have the smallest of everything because I like to think big. Cute, right? Put a little smile on your face, maybe? I buy stuff online and I make it if I can't find it. It could be anything, from tables and chairs to army tanks and train sets. I've got the *biggest* collection of *tiny* things this side of the country. That fact alone normally gives people something to laugh about considering my day job…

I'm the elephant keeper at Dublin Zoo. If it wasn't for my elephants I think I would've curled up in my shell a long time ago and wait for the slow, steady decline towards my end. Thank Christ I've got a job that keeps me going! So there's that for starters, but let me just tell you that there's one elephant in particular that is my shoulder to cry on: Sinbad.

Sinbad is a four-tonne, forty-two year-old Indian bull-elephant that started out his days at the zoo with my old man and was handed down to me. *That's* the special thing I mentioned a few lines back; it's the living thread that connects me with the spirit of my old man. It's this very special thing which keeps me sane, for want of a better word, during these dark times… I can put my hand on my heart and tell you that Sinbad is my best friend. If anything were to happen to him, well, I'd be alone in this world. Sinbad listens to me – he is the perfect psychiatrist because he likes to listen and doesn't charge.

Sinbad was just a few years old when my father retired. I remember the day he was born at the zoo. I was fifteen years old and I was helping my father one Saturday (shovelling dung was my main chore). That was the day I learned the reality of the birds and the bees – the messy end of it, at least. I thought Sinbad's mother had left her insides outside when she gave birth to Sinbad, but apparently it was only the afterbirth. I'd never seen anything so evil and disgusting in my young life…

Sorry, I'm doing it again…give me a dig in the ribs when I start going on about the good old days… You see, Reader, I can't remember what happened yesterday, but I *can* tell you what happened twenty years ago…

I'm hiding an illness – a big illness and it's got a lot to do with memory and memories. So all this fluffy jiving on about my past *does* have significance: I've got Alzheimer's. There, it's out there.

Nobody knows about it; only the doctor who gave me the results, and I'm just a number to him. So don't tell anybody, okay? *Especially* at work. I won't tell anybody about the Alzheimer's until I have to. I should tell the bosses, but if I lose my job, I lose the will to live…Dramatic? No. I've still got another five years till my retirement at the zoo and I *can't* afford, economically and spiritually, to take early retirement so it's a secret for now. Zip it!

Lately, just once or twice, I've had funny turns (not so funny) where routines I've had for twenty years are suddenly new to me and it's like seeing somebody else's routine. And my short-term memory is shot to pieces, hence the Post-It invasion at my place. My intention is to go on being Mick Munroe.

Now, before you tell me off for dumbing down a serious Illness. *I'm* the one with the serious illness and humour is my best defence, so humour me.

Now, if you'll excuse me, I'm off to make a throne fit for an ant-king.

The Zoo

Hello, you've caught me on a work day. Seeing as you're here, I might as well show you around…

My day starts out at the zoo by shovelling great heaps of shit as a new parent might clean up a baby's behind. It may be fifty times more, but give me elephant dung any day – I've seen what some babies leave behind when their grub doesn't agree with them. Oh, mercy!

Once the cleaning-out is done with, I feed Sinbad and the others their daily ration of hay (and a Snickers which I sneak into the zoo, which isn't really good for Sinbad, but we've all got our vices and mine includes smoking, though I'm not ashamed to say it). Sinbad loves his Snickers and didn't have any problem adapting from Marathon (Snickers' previous name).

While Sinbad and the others are having breakfast, I like to play traditional Indian music on the battered old CD player that I've got hidden in a place where their wandering trunks can't get to. The strings of Ravi Shankar's Indian sitar seem to have a soothing effect over my elephants, especially Sinbad who is the eldest (the oldest elephant in Ireland, I'm led to believe). Twangy notes echo out around their concrete-and-steel enclosure and whisper of their forefathers' desert-and-jungle subcontinent. Management has warned me against the music for Health & Safety reasons, but that's why I do it – for the health and safety of my elephants. Nobody knows Sinbad like I do and I've seen how he reacts to Shankar's mystic music. Only somebody who has spent four decades or so with an elephant can see these little nuances, mainly because the animals are so big and that's the first thing that people notice when they're up close with an elephant: BIG. But keepers like me see the little signs, and I can read how he is feeling just by how Sinbad looks at me. I've heard about some police departments speaking to their German Shepherds in German and French Poodles in French, but I think this is taking it a little far – do the dogs bark in German or French? But I would agree with Beethoven or Debussy being played to them in their kennels at night.

These days I tend to talk more and more to Sinbad and use him as a substitute for Gloria. I'm not comparing Gloria to an Indian elephant, but she *was* just as big in my life. As I said, he's my occasional shoulder to cry on. He understands; I can see it in his eyes. That may sound like bullshit, but it's not. Trust me. He knows; he can pick up my vibes. Sinbad stays clear on days when I'm angry at the world, how it just sat by and watched my wife fade away, not that I would ever harm a wiry bristle on his head.

Once Sinbad is taken care of, I normally go to the keepers' hut where we drink tea, eat from Tupperware, smoke, chat, and puff some more. It's our home-away-from-home, and there is no smoking ban when top brass isn't milling around.

This is where I am now, Reader.

Come in and take a plastic chair; the first one you find that doesn't have a whoopie-cushion hidden somewhere on it because one of our keepers is an amateur comedian and I *mean* amateur. He's so amateur he's actually funny.

So, just sit back and enjoy the bullshit, that's what I like to do.

'So here's my itinerary: we're going to take a flight from Dublin to Amsterdam, and from there we're going to cross over into Belgium, then we…'

Smiler, (that's the guy reading from an itinerary with a magnifying glass because only his left eye is weak, and he's too cheap to fork out for a pair of glasses) is the monkey-man around here, the monkey keeper, and Smiler (AKA George Gillespie, though I can't remember when I last used that name aloud) has always got a slight, knowing

smile on his face no matter the circumstances and we *can't*
overlook the glint in his eye that could be mistaken for a
squint. And y'know what? I think he does 'know'. Smiler,
always cool as a breeze. He's obsessed with itineraries,
especially when nobody else in the keepers' hut is
interested. And he's got a talent for making Ryanair
European tourist destinations sound like unexplored, virgin
territory, like he just did with "cross over into Belgium..."
as if he had slipped the border-patrol a grubby 50 and
sneaked into the country.

But Smiler is a good buddy, and we've put down thirty
years together at the zoo and we've seen it
all. Some of the keepers say that we've spent too much
time with the animals which has left us socially inept. It's a
joke, like everything else in the hut, but sometimes I
happen to think they're right. I *do* think that Smiler spends
far too much time with the orang-utans. But to be fair, he is
having marital problems – apparently Kelly isn't so what-
you-see-is-what-you-get. If I have to say one bad thing
about Smiler it would probably be that he doesn't think
twice about scratching his privates in public like you and I
would do the first thing in the morning in the privacy of our
bathroom. On other occasions, I've witnessed him
siphoning through his hair as a chimpanzee would. The
next step will be siphoning the other keepers' hair. I've
seen him staring at heads, *wanting* to have a good dig
around in the follicles for foreign bodies. Smiler is
legitimate proof that we do come from monkeys.

'...and then down to Berlin where we will hire one of
the locals...'

Having said that, Smiler is my second best friend and the
only thing he doesn't know about me is that I'm on the
verge of forgetting everything, including myself, and *that*,
dear Reader, is a frightening prospect. But what's more
terrifying is that I forget myself, but I continue being Mick
Munroe to everybody else; they will see my decline until I

am a stranger. They will know me when I don't know me. That idea is unnerving.

Smiler continues his itinerary when suddenly, I get the unsettling feeling that I don't know where I am. No, unsettling is too mild for what I'm feeling. *Scared*, that's how I'm feeling. I look around the hut. I *know* I've been here before, but I just can't place it, like I've seen it in a dream. I'm frozen to my chair, afraid to get up, speak, and equally dreading somebody (one of these strangers) speaking to me. I *know* I know them, but it's like a face that passes on the street – you know you've seen that face before, but for the life of you, you can't tell you where…

'Mick?'

'Huh?'

Smiler looks at me. 'You're lookin' a little lost there. Gazin' off into space, like…'

I wave it off. 'I've just remembered that I left the TV on.'

I have no idea who this guy is…

That excuse seems to go down well with the man with the magnifying glass, so he settles back on his paperwork. I lean in to get a better look to see what it is he is doing. Maybe it'll jog my memory. I see something hand-written about   an   itinerary   of   some kind…destinations…places…times.

I sit tight and try to relax and pretend there's nothing wrong. The more I relax, the better I am and within seconds, I'm back in the room, as the hypnotist might say.

These forgetful bouts are happening more frequently, but it's nothing the doctors haven't warned me about. I started getting these suspended bouts of animation in November, last year.

Look, Reader, now that I have my wits about me, let me introduce you to the rest of the team before I start getting bogged down in something I don't really want to talk about

– I know Bob Hoskins says *it's good to talk*, but Bob isn't the one with Alzheimer's...

That scrawny, red-faced guy with the sandy hair is Birdman. You've probably deducted what section of the zoo he cares for. His real name is Mitchell, but it's Birdman around here. If you're ever walking behind him, be sure to check out his mean penguin imitation. He walks along with this stiff gait and a slight bob to the left and right. I think his posture is due to an accident, but everybody 'round here often brings up the old *Puh-Puh-Puh-Penguin* TV ad. No mercy in the hut.

That woman sitting over there by herself with the big, frizzy hair and face like a fish works in, yeah, you guessed, the aquarium. Doesn't she look like a fish with those big, ogling eyes and those lips? It's not too hard to imagine her looking out at you from one of the aquarium tanks. We call her Goldie (Fishwoman seemed inappropriate). She likes to play cards and when nobody wants to play, she deals herself and her imaginary opponent a hand. That's what she's doing now. She doesn't find many opponents here in the hut because she tends to complain about every fucking subject under the sun. I tend not to engage her in conversation about crooked politicians because I feel that I'm wasting my breath. There were crooked politicians in the time of Christ and there will be more of them when Hell freezes over.

'Goldie's playing with herself again!'

And bang on-cue; that guy who just made that wise observation is Larry T or Whiskers to you and me. That's right, Whiskers works with the big cats, though I think he sees himself on a Las Vegas stage. Whiskers is an amateur stand-up comedian who can sometimes be found on the dingier stages of Dublin City. The thing is, he's so unfunny that he's funny. The guy is funny. But, like his cats, approach with caution as Whiskers tends to have bouts of severe depression. Then his jokes are not so funny. You've caught him on one of his good days... Just yesterday Whiskers confided in me that, sometimes, he feels so insignificant that automatic doors don't open for him. And if he ever contemplated suicide then he couldn't think of a better way to blow out the candle than offering himself up to his big cats in some kind of reincarnation thing (not unlike our backyard apple tree). But it really bugs him not knowing if his cats would or wouldn't eat him. "I've heard that dogs don't eat their owners, but domestic cats would."

Reader, you may think that all of this is just fluff, filling out the pages. Well, you'd be wrong. What I'm trying to show you is that this bunch of miscreants is the only thing going on in my life now. I've got my elephant of course, but Sinbad's an Indian elephant, see what I mean? Outside this zoo, I don't have much.

I light up a cigarette.

'Those things will kill you,' says Goldie, not taking her eyes off her imaginary opponent. 'I'm tired of saying it.'

'I could also get killed crossing the street outside...'

'Chances are slim and it is only a chance, but those things cut years off.'

Whiskers kicks in, 'My postman smoked forty on his route every day, always a ciggie sticking out from the corner of his lip, sometimes lit, sometimes a dog-end. He lived till he was 95. Always a stench of smoke off the post...'

'He would've lived to 105 if he hadn't smoked,' back-answers Goldie. 'You should smoke one of those electric cigarettes, Mick...'

'And you should drink non-alcohol beer, Goldie,' I answer back.

It's time to go back to work. I leave the hut and carry on with my chores for the next few hours and then my working day comes to an end, which I've already covered. The last of the visitors vacate the zoo and the zoo gates are locked. The rest of the crew go home, but I'm going to stay on here a little while longer and just sit with my elephant and listen to Ravi Shankar.

How Forgetfulness can't be Forgotten

Who needs a phone-call at four in the morning? Nobody, but I still get one, Reader.

Sorry that I'd never connected up a bedside phone (Gloria never liked the idea, saying that it would scare her out of her wits if it ever rang, LIKE NOW).

I stumble downstairs with my shook, old heart hammering in my ears and temples. The distance from the top of the stairs to the hallway seems to take a life-time and I wonder who can be ringing me? But more importantly, why? Reader, who might be ringing you at this ungodly hour? I bet the first thing that comes to you is family, right? Bad news in the family. Well, I've got none, so that eliminates a lot right there. I had a brother, but he died young under general anaesthetic: a "simple" hospital procedure – tonsils. The only consolation we had at the time was that he left us peacefully, and I quake in my boots every time I hear about somebody going in for a "simple" procedure.

But now is not the time to be taking the violins out of their cases because that phone is still ringing…

'Hello?' I make a quick note on a nearby Post-It to get one of those caller-ID thingamajigs.

A voice booms down the line at me. *'Elephant!'* The owner of the voice struggles and spits out *'Elephant!!!'* again.

'Who is this?' Stupid question; I already know who it is.

'It's the *elephant!!*'

This is getting confusing. 'Sorry? I don't…'

'Mick, this is Smiler! Your *fucking* elephant is rampaging across Phoenix Park with its trunk pointing towards India!! The fire-service is down here right now trying to get the situation under control! In a strange kind

16

of way, it's almost beautiful to watch – the elephant breaking free of his cage and heading back
to the wilds of India. A noble cause.' There's a pause on the line. 'But there's nothing noble about the rifle the police have just turned up with…'

I can barely process what I'm hearing. My mind picks up the mega-bytes and jumbles them into its own beautiful logic: *There's an elephant on fire in a park in India…*

Things must be desperate; Smiler isn't big on romanticism, but it breaks my heart just the same. 'Oh mercy,' is all I manage to mutter before I grow dizzy and collapse on the floor. 'Which one?'

'The big one! Does it matter, Mick? I mean, does it *really* matter?! A loose elephant is a loose elephant in my book!'

What's more frightening about all of this is Smiler's face down the other end of the line. I can tell, just by the way he's speaking, he has lost that eternal, twinkling smirk of his. 'Smiler, which ele–'

'Sinbad! It's Sinbad!'

Nerves flutter inside me on hearing my elephant's name…It would have to be Sinbad, wouldn't it, Reader.

'*Somebody* left his gate open. I wonder who could that be?! A little mouse, *maybe?!* Shit-fire, Mick, shit-fire! You need to get down here to Phoenix Park right now and call off your elephant! He's done some damage around the zoo and do you remember the little kids park by the restaurant!?'

'Where?'

'On Mars, Mick. The *zooooooo!*'

All I can manage is 'Uh-huh…'

'Exactly…*remember*. It's been obliterated. I think Sinbad tried to go down the slide!'

I almost snigger. So many things are going through my mind right now, but coming to the fore of all these rushing images is one pulsing realization: this was an accident

17

waiting to happen. It was only a matter of time before I slipped up. I haven't told anybody – not even Smiler – that I have left Sinbad's gate open once already. It happened two weeks ago, and it was only luck that he didn't go sniffing around his gate. Please, don't tell anybody, Reader.

In the background, I hear Sinbad's wild trumpeting like I've never heard it before…but it's him; I'd know Sinbad's call anywhere. He sounds distressed. I know he's looking for me. Or is he? Maybe he just wants out. He cannot believe his luck. He's got the taste of freedom now –

'Mick! Hell*ooooo!*'

'I'm coming. Gimme two minutes…'

'Make it one minute cos the police…'

Trembling, I hang up five or six times before the phone in my shaking hand fits into its cradle, vaguely hearing the rest of Smiler's words.

I scramble back upstairs, now trying to recall when I'd left Sinbad's enclosure just a few hours ago. I had stayed till after nine pm, chatting idly with Sinbad as I've done on numerous nights. Tim Long, zoo director and long-time friend, allows me to stay on a little late on the sly because he knows my home situation is dismal. Then I switched out the lights, locked the gate, said good-night to Gerry 'The Berry', the night security-man, and came home. I'm only presuming I did that, but I *can't* actually remember leaving the zoo. The question is, did I have one of my black-outs then or not? Or maybe I was fine, but now I can't remember? Chicken or the egg? I can see my routine, but I can't recall any of it after switching out Sinbad's light, not really. It's like I've drunk too much and completely forgotten the sequence of events after leaving Sinbad to settle down for the night. I know I've been increasingly forgetful, but a whole chunk of an evening has just fizzled out forever.

I pull on my keeper uniform over my pyjamas. I grab a couple of on-standby Snickers from the fridge, throw on my anorak and trilby (which caused some raised eyebrows and giggles when I first started wearing it from the mentally-challenged members of our zoo fraternity), then roll out into the freezing night, and sit into my battered old Renault Clio…

And that's where the break-neck speed of this chapter stops, Reader, because my Renault Clio doesn't want to start. I'd laugh if I was watching myself on a telly screen. The car chugs and splutters. It's been neglected like this for months and I know exactly when to floor the accelerator, so I do so and an unmerciful puff of black smoke explodes from the back of the car. That means the engine is now running and Clio is happy to take me somewhere…

Ten minutes later, I pull into the zoo's employee car park. I switch off the engine, roll down the window, light up a cigarette to qualm my quaking nerves, and listen out into the night. Phoenix Park is a big area, almost 1800 acres, and I'm racking my befuddled brain, trying to figure out where my elephant might be.

I get out and sit on the bonnet. For a moment there is nothing, but then I hear him – Sinbad – in the distance. It's surreal to hear his trumpeting calls from outside the confines of the zoo and, I have to admit, Reader, it's a beautiful thing. A part of me wants to let him run…and run…and *never* look back. Maybe I'd like to do the same.

I cross the car-park and enter Phoenix Park. I follow my elephant's blaring calls in the night, dragging on my cigarette like it's my last one and cursing to high heavens, quoting my favourite swear-word in heated moments as I run across the grass: *'Fucking moron!'* Me, not the elephant.

Five minutes cross-country, I come upon a sight that I know I will *never* forget despite my impending illness. For a suspended moment in time, the world becomes mute and slow-motion. I witness the swirling emergency lights, the firemen and police dancing around Sinbad with dread and fear etched in their puppet-faces. They're losing the battle. Men jump in and out of the lights and back into shadows. What are they trying to capture him with? It seems that they're attempting to corner him with ladders and trip him up with hoses. They're out of their depth…

Smiler is there too, standing out of harm's way and he isn't smiling anymore, but more disbelief – an expression that could say: *Just go back to sleep, Smiler, it's all just a dream…*

Maybe it is; maybe it isn't.

In this very moment, despite consequences, I am delighted for Sinbad – he doesn't know what it is to be free. Seeing my friend is heart-breaking, but also enlightening. Smiler had been right; there is something noble about Sinbad's escape. It's a mix of emotions, but more heart-rending than anything because he is revelling in this brief ray of hope outside his concrete walls. I want to let him be free and take his chances…

I almost turn away (nobody has seen me yet), but I cannot turn my back on my old friend. He doesn't know where he is or what's going on, and the lights have confused and angered him. He's disorientated and I feel the same. 'Somebody's going to get killed!' I roar. 'Sinbad!' I call out. 'C'mon, boy! Come get yer Snickers!'

Sinbad suddenly stalls and looks sharply in my direction along with half of Dublin's fire-service *and* police.

'Get the lights out of his face!' I yell. 'He can't see where he's going! He'll trample one of you!'

Smiler shouts, 'Do what he says!'

It's a mild comfort to see him here, but the terror on his face is almost worse than any of this. The emergency services don't appear to believe or listen to Smiler.

Smiler clarifies: 'Jesus Christ! He's the elephant-keeper at the zoo…Mick Munroe…'

This time they do understand and do as I ask.

I call my elephant again and Sinbad comes directly for me at top speed, ears flapping.

For a brief moment, I think I'm going to be killed by my own elephant. *'Sinbad, it's me!'*

He diverts at the last moment and manages to pick the bar of chocolate out of my hand with his trunk, curls it down into his gaping mouth, before coming to a stop. He savours his favourite snack before shaking his great, hulking head in disapproval at the law-makers' negotiating tactics.

One of the fire-fighters shouts, '*Now* what?'

'Yeah, *now* what?' Smiler echoes.

I give Sinbad a few more seconds of freedom before putting the men out of their misery by reluctantly coaxing my elephant with another Snickers across the dewy Phoenix Park. Tremors of adrenaline and bald fear lace through me *and* infinite sadness because now I have to lock him up and *now* he knows what it is to be free.

But Sinbad refuses to move, like a spoilt child. I wave the Snickers in his face and roll it in my hand, making sounds with the wrapper. He doesn't budge until I sternly command: 'Come!'

Then he decides to follow me, in no great hurry. I instruct the others to light our way back to the zoo.

Thankfully, during our forty years together, I've taught Sinbad basic one-word instructions: 'Come...' 'Go...' 'Push...' 'Pull...'

As we cross the grass, I decide that it's time to face up to my condition, and by that, I mean not keeping it a secret anymore. I'm becoming a liability. Next time could be worse.

Human (without) Resources

The following morning, it comes as no surprise that I am called into the Human Resources Department during my coffee-break at the keepers' hut. Dare I say that I am even relieved to find an excuse to get out of the hut? Never thought I'd say it, Reader, but the atmosphere in there was getting a tad uncomfortable. The other keepers are a little off with me, even Smiler's giving me the cold shoulder. They try to persuade me that "anybody could leave a gate open" yet none of them have ever done it. I *know* they're trying to stand by me, but I feel the tension, especially when Sinbad damaged a few of the other enclosures in his rush to get to Phoenix Park. Not to mention the stress caused to their animals seeing another animal finally make a prison-break.

The zoo manager, Tim Long, is sitting in the HR office with a face as long as his surname, along with two other women from HR sitting either side of him. The one on Long's left is the HR boss, a notorious highly-strung, but never strung highly enough, mid-50's divorced bitch. I won't do her justice by mentioning her name, but I'm sure it'll come out sooner or later. I'm not familiar with the other woman. I've known Tim since he was a teenager. We normally sit at the same table for the Christmas staff dinner and always have something meaningful to talk about. However, his demeanour this morning is different. He looks like a worried man, more than me, if that's possible.

I sit myself down and nod a curt *good morning*. I'm nervous, really quaking in my boots. Today is the day – right now – when I reveal my big secret to the world.

'Michael,' Long kicks off using my proper name which is formal and worrying. He reads from his notes while not meeting my gaze, totally out of character, 'we all know why we're here. Nobody, uh, can ignore the elephant in the room…'

One of the women looks at Tim Long in disdain, disgust, or confusion, don't know which, maybe all. The other younger woman smiles and sniffs.

'There was, um, an *occurrence* last night at the elephant enclosure – *outside it*, more like.' Long speaks like a lawyer would, outlining the crime scene to a stern judge. 'One elephant in particular, named Sinbad, apparently walked free from his enclosure and proceeded down the main zoo thoroughfare without a care in the world, *found* an opening and let himself out among the general public of Dublin City. I correct myself,' Long corrects his notes, 'the elephant *created* an opening in the main gates by running *through* them. Along the way, Sinbad caused a few thousand Euros worth of damage, plus other miscellaneous damages…'

'The coke machine…' the woman on the right of Tim Long clarifies. 'Visitors have been helping themselves to free cans of Fanta and Lilt all morning.'

The woman on the other side of Long leans across and looks at her colleague. '*Lilt?* I didn't know that even existed anymore.'

'It's a *great* drink…'

It could be an advertisement for Lilt.

Long interjects, 'Let's just stick to the subject matter.'

I comment, 'They should be careful when they open the cans – fizz…' I mime opening an exploding can, but regret it at the same time. I put it down to nerves.

'Mick, this isn't a laughing matter. Dympna just happened to point out the, um, Coke machine, but that's the least of my worries. My worry is that our insurance premium has just gone through the roof. Visitor numbers are dropping; parents are looking at the zoo like they would at a circus. They're going out of their way to find wildlife parks these days where the fence is a little further away and

23

hidden. Then we have to deal with the negative press on top of that. Mick, what happened last night?'

'Smiler rang me around four this morning and told me that –'

'No, I mean, before that; what led up to the fact that Sinbad went for a stroll in Phoenix Park?'

The lesser of the two HR dragons, Dympna, finds the whole thing very amusing and makes no
attempt to hide her sniggers.

Long cannot contain himself. 'Jesus, Mick, Sinbad could've trampled somebody.'

I back-answer, 'I can think of one or two –'

The HR boss cuts in. 'This isn't the time for jokes, Michael. What if...'

'*If...*' I stop her. 'We're talking about something that hasn't happened. *Nobody* was hurt.'

'It's true,' the other HR representative pipes up, 'the only people that'd get trampled at that hour of the morning are the drug addicts and bums in the park and who will miss – '

The HR Evil Queen answers back, 'I went there after-hours and it wasn't to take drugs.' She raises her eyebrows, suggesting a number of possibilities, but the most likely being of a carnal nature. 'I was younger, let's leave it at that. So imagine that and having an elephant sneak up on you when you're…'

The other whispers, 'Perve…'

'How about a little professionalism, girls?' Long isn't enjoying any of this.

Meanwhile, I'm beginning to sweat because these ladies don't understand animals. They work with papers all day and couldn't possibly imagine the relationship I have with Sinbad. Maybe one of them has a poodle, but that's about it. Now is a good a time as any to tell the truth. 'I'm too long in the tooth now to bullshit anybody and the chances are I'd more than likely forget my story anyway – I do have some dignity left.'

There's a pause. In this pause, three confused faces look at me.

'I can't remember what happened last night. Smiler told me that I left Sinbad's gate unlocked, but I've no recollection of it.' I pause before speaking my next few words; words that will change everything: 'I've got Alzheimer's.'

The three shocked faces in front of me exchange glances that tell me that this was the last thing they were expecting. I reach inside my overalls pocket and hand over the devastatingly simple page of hospital test results to Long; nothing more than a ticked box next to *'...Alzheimer's'*.

After a prolonged silence, Long's first reaction is to stare at the results, unblinking, lost for words. He then skips over it quickly and nods, as if everything makes sense now. He hands it to the HR honcho on his right who looks at the test results in more detail, donning the pair of red spectacles dangling from her neck; one of those modern, magnet types that can be opened and shut. I prefer the old chain myself.

Long speaks, 'I'm very sorry to hear this. Since when, Mick?'

'Since they gave me the results last September. It's dated at the top.' I gesture to the page.

'Last *September?* You should've told us sooner.'

Tears surprise me. 'I know. I just…I just needed something to hold onto after Gloria passed – some normality in my life that would ground me. My job is everything to me – *more* than a job.'

Long nods. 'I met Gloria every Christmas at the zoo dos. She was one hell of a lady, Mick. She's sorely missed.'

'I love my job and would do nothing to endanger it…'

'Except let an elephant loose…'

Tim Long throws a disbelieving glance at the vindictive bitch to his right, but not enough to jeopardize his position.

Even Dympna isn't so sure anymore.

'What?' she asks defensively, 'What did I say that isn't true, Tim?'

'How about showing a little compassion?' Long turns to me. 'Who else have you told?'

I shake my head. That's my answer.

The frowns in the room cause consternation. The woman to Long's left asks sympathetically, 'You were diagnosed with Alzheimer's disease seven months ago and you've told *nobody?*'

'I told Sinbad.'

Long raises his eyebrows in an expression that says: *Oh, bollocks, I'm on your side, Mick, but giving us pearls like that…* Almost as if I've just let him down in front of HR.

The woman to Long's left sees her boss's reaction. 'Who is Sinbad anyway?'

I can't believe she doesn't even know we've got the oldest elephant in the country and one of the biggest stars at the zoo.

'The elephant,' her HR boss answers. 'What have we been talking about for the last ten minutes?' Long is annoyed. 'Have you been listening to anything?'

Dympna reddens and hides her face in some paperwork.

The HR boss speaks from her inner sanctum to Long and her protégée. 'I think that this is an appropriate juncture to temporarily wind-up proceedings.' She says it on one breath, obviously a phrase she has used before.

The zoo manager takes that as his cue to speak in English to me. 'Mick, we're going to take a little break. I need to speak with a few people about this situation. This changes everything, you realize that?'

'Yes.' I feel a little calmer now; a sense of relief. But now there's a new bubble of nerves swelling inside me. At least they know that there's a good (or bad) reason behind leaving Sinbad's gate open.

'Mick, go for a coffee or whatever and meet us back here at,' checks his watch, 'mid-day.' He looks at the others for their approval and they give it unwillingly.

I nod and make my way from the office with six eyes searing into the back of my head, trying to see the illness hidden inside my skull in the form of a clouded MRI image.

My mind is going into overdrive, Reader. Sudden, irrational fear grips me as I leave the HR building. Maybe it hadn't been such a good idea to tell them about my illness. But I had no choice, had I? What would you have done, Reader? This is going to back-fire. I should've kept my mouth shut and just owned up to leaving the gate open. What was the sense in telling them that I was ill? The sense is that I was hoping that they might take pity on me. I even mentioned Gloria...

Reader, here is something that I *hate* about myself: I find I seek pity by giving the excuse of Gloria's death so people will feel *sorry* for me. When any serious issue comes up and I'm to blame, I spin the old 'Gloria passed away recently and I haven't been thinking clearly...' That excuse only goes so far, especially two years later. It's as if Gloria has been degraded to nothing but a handy excuse for pity. Oh, mercy. What a snivelling, little old man I am.

Maybe I'm just over-reacting. Maybe HR and Long have some kind of master-plan that will help with the situation. That's probably it...

I find Smiler all alone in the hut, working on one of his itineraries. Now is as good a time as any: rumours travel fast at the zoo, especially in the exotic bird enclosure where macaws and mynahs repeat secrets, word for word. I don't jest; it has happened in the past.

I pull up a chair next to my friend. He doesn't acknowledge me as usual, with his nose and magnifying-glass stuck in his travel plans. He starts going on about some sight-seeing in the city of Valencia on the Spanish

Coast and the possibility of getting to know the locals and their strange customs and traditions. My mind is far away from Valencia right now as I contemplate how to come at the subject of Alzheimer's. I try to blurt it out: *I have Alzheimer's, so now you know and let that be the end of it...* 'I was, um, reading an interesting article on Alzheimer's the other day.' *Not bad, go on...*

'Oh, yeah?' Smiler doesn't look up from his dangerous route into virgin orange-growing Valencian territory.

'That's that forgetting disease, right?' Smiler chuckles to himself. 'Anybody would think you have it, the rate you're carrying on at here. I'd get myself checked...'

...if I were you are Smiler's words that go unspoken because he has just read between the lines of the imaginary article that I supposedly read. He pauses, looking *through* his magic glass and magnifying this horrible situation. He looks up and studies me through his mega monocle. It scares me to see his smirk-dimple drop from his face. 'Mick?'

It's the same face I saw last night when Sinbad was free.

I purse my lips and sigh, mentally trying to down-size this mental problem I have.

'Michael, is everything okay?'

'Don't call me Michael, George.'

Smiler knows that everything *isn't* okay; he wouldn't have called me Michael otherwise. His gut reaction is to ask the same question Long had asked me, I know it, but he keeps his mouth shut and lets me do the talking.

So I talk...and I talk...

I tell Smiler *everything*, it comes gushing out of me, all those pent-up emotions, feelings, words that have gone unspoken far too long. And all I can think about is my elephant. I think Sinbad is a defence mechanism, does that make sense, Reader?

Smiler is speechless and seems to go into a trance for a few moments. He looks around the table for answers that don't come. His eyes widen and he nods as Tim Long had done before him. 'That explains everything,' he says on a cryptic note. Then repeats himself. 'I was a little worried, to be honest with you. You've left a string of accidents behind you.' He nods again, mentally joining the dots. 'I knew there was something up, but never this...You had me worried.' Stalls. 'Now I see I've got reason to worry...'

'A string of accidents?'

Smiler waves it away. 'Ah, forget it.'

'No, tell me. By the way, could you put down the magnifying-glass? I feel like an itinerary.'

Smiler reddens and laughs, diffusing the situation a little. 'Just general zoo-code shit that was forgotten. You're normally meticulous. That's not important now, but what is important is why you didn't tell me sooner?'

'What'd be the point of that? I have it; it's not going away. Who needs that negativity?'

'Jesus, Mick, what's the *point?!* I could've covered your ass with this loose elephant business for one. I would've thought of *something*. I would've taken the fall for you.'

Smiler surprises me. I was thinking in more general terms, like the fact that I've got Alzheimer's. I'm not sure what he's getting at. He seems more concerned about Sinbad escaping than my general state of health. Anybody would think he has more on his agenda. 'Smiler, we're not a couple of kids anymore. It's about time I faced up to this and maybe leaving Sinbad's gate open is just the medicine I need. Seeing him free like that has given me a new lease of life.'

Smiler huffs a weak chuckle.

'I'm not joking. It has...*stirred*...something inside me. I felt what my elephant felt.'

'A bit like Elliott and E.T....'

'Huh?'

Smiler is about to answer back when my walkie-talkie crackles.

'Mick, would you mind passing by the office.'

Smiler lip-synchs: *Fuck!*

'After work?'

'No, now.' Pause. 'Um, now would be a good time for us.'

Another *Fuck* from Smiler.

I don't like the sound of this and neither does Smiler, judging by his frown.

I leave Smiler to his melancholic thoughts and itineraries and saunter back up to the office.

The three of them are sitting there with glummer faces than when I had left.

Tim Long avoids making eye-contact. 'Mick, I've known you many years…'

Here we go…

'And I know you're not a man to beat around the bush so I'll respect that and tell you outright the situation that we've got on our hands.' He pauses. 'We've taken everything into consideration and we feel…' Long's emotions are getting the best of him now; his mouth is beginning to twist. 'I mean, on a personal level, I've known you a long time and um…'

The HR dragon clears her throat to speak, but Long side-glances her and continues this torturous meeting. Sinbad free and majestic in Phoenix Park flashes before my eyes…

'We feel that it's best for all – including Sinbad – if you would hang-up your keeper overalls. We think it's a good time to retire, Mick. You need to start taking care of yourself.'

This is the worst news I could receive. I feel faint and, for a second, I think I'm only imagining this. I'm sitting here, but nobody has said anything yet.

'I'm sorry,' Long apologises, tearing me from my moment of surrealism.

'But I'm only sixty. I've got five more years in me…'

'We'd like to offer you this generous redundancy package.' Long doesn't listen to me. 'It's a good time to retire, Mick.' Long nods; a nod that says all of this has already been decided.

I refuse to take the document from Long, who, if my eyes don't deceive me, is welling up. Maybe he had a raw onion for breakfast, but I don't think so.

Long sighs and eyes the HR women. 'Don't make this difficult, Mick.'

The woman on the right speaks without compassion, but speaks the truth. 'Sinbad could've been hurt. You could've been hurt. Anybody out for a midnight stroll in Phoenix Park could've gotten a rude awakening.'

'Uh-huh.' I'm slipping into a cold paralysis.

Long breaks the silence. 'Do it for your elephant if not for yourself.'

Dympna regrets her little quip already. 'Do it for the kids.'

'Are you asking me or telling me to take early retirement?'

The three exchange glances before Long hammers the final nail into my coffin (and I do feel closer to it now, Reader). 'We're telling you, Mick. I'm sorry.'

The HR woman on Long's right speaks: 'You're too much of a liability, Michael, and we *know* this isn't the first time you've slipped up.'

Dympna nods her approval at her boss's words.

Long interrupts, 'It is all water under the bridge now, Deirdre. Let's just leave it there and move on.'

Deirdre's her name…

'No,' I chime in, 'I'm *not* going to *leave* it there. I'd like to know what inside info *Deirdre* has on me.'

Why can't I forget where I am now, Reader? Just like at the keepers' hut yesterday or was it the day before? Alzheimer's isn't funny, but if ever I wished it would take me temporarily to the land of Forget-me-Not then it is right here, right now.

Without needing to locate her information, crow No.1, 'Deirdre', clears her throat and begins reading from a list of minor occurrences that have involved me during the last two months. They all involve forgetting something with resulting hazardous dangers (that never happen) and it's all true.

Who told her?

'Okay,' I admit, 'so there were one or two other minor things other than leaving Sinbad's gate open that might've skipped my mind, but you'll forgive me. Where did you get this information?'

'Never mind.'

I sum up the situation by saying, 'Snake in the grass, eh?'

'It *is* a zoo,' answers Dympna with remarkable insight.

'Your speciality seems to be setting animals free,' opines Deirdre, glimpsing down at her papers. 'We never found that snake, by the way.'

Dympna giggles for her boss's pleasure.

'But it'll come up somebody's lavatory and bite them on the ass, and then we'll find the goddamn thing along with an insurance claim stuck on its forked tongue.'

Long throws a look at me that says: *these are a regular couple of vipers...*

I ask again, 'Who's the spy?'

'We've got our sources. Actually, it's common knowledge, Mick. The sad fact is that...'

Long stares at Deirdre in an attempt to shut her up, but she just has to bring everybody else down to her level to have that *feel-good* buzz about herself.

I speak my mind to Tim. 'It's plain to see who's wearing the trousers around this office despite you being the zoo manager.'

'One of your colleagues came to us a fortnight ago and recommended we relieve you of your duties because he...'

'...*or* she...' interjects Dympna.

'*Or* she...is worried that you will end up hurting yourself, one of the animals, or somebody else. And God forbid, a visitor. You've been leaving pitch-forks in dangerous places where kids play and several members of staff have locked gates after you. The list goes on, Mick, and your elephant breaking out last night was the straw that broke the camel's back – and you *will* break the camel's back at the rate you're going.'

'One hump or two?' asks Dympna, unable to hold in the snigger. 'My husband, Landon,' she tells me, 'asks me that every time we have a coffee.' Then she goes quiet again. 'Hilarious.'

I suddenly plead, 'Tim, don't do this! I'll clean up my act.'

Long shakes his head despondently. 'Mick, it's not about cleaning up your act. You're the finest keeper we've ever had at the zoo, but there has been a noticeable change during the last six months, and now I know why and I'm relieved that it's the Alzheimer's. That came out wrong, but I think you know what I mean. You have a legitimate reason to retire with your head held high.'

'Please, I'll work for nothing to pay off whatever this has cost you.' A sudden flash of being at home and listening to the tick-tock of my grandfather clock in the silence cuts me deep and sharp. 'Don't take my elephant away from me!'

It almost sounds comical, but I weep and with that comes an outpouring of home truths. I tell the three faces that I'm all alone – it's not a sympathy vote, but the damn truth. No, sorry it *is* a sympathy vote because I'm at it again, am I not, Reader? My boo-hoo story – *please feel sorry for me because my wife died...* Jesus, if you're going to feel sorry for anyone, feel sorry for Gloria! My Glow is lying in the ground!

'This zoo is my life, Tim, you know that.' I'm struggling to keep my composure now. Dread, *real* fucking dread, starts to manifest in beads of sweat on my forehead. I grow all clammy and nauseous and resort to history to save me. 'You knew my old man was a keeper before me…'

'And a good one, like yourself...' Long stalls, as if he's about to give me a second chance. He looks at the others with that raised-eyebrow thing, but he is met by a hard wall, I see it, we can all see it.

For a tiny moment there, I was almost hopeful…

'Sorry, Mick, the decision has been taken. As from now, and with regret, you are no longer the elephant-keeper at Dublin Zoo. It's tough to say this. Deirdre brought up a few things here I was hoping she'd keep to herself, but she's got the bones of this right – you have to go.' Long smiles, but it's costing him. 'Mick, we were that close,' displaying a smidgen of air between his thumb and forefinger, 'from being sued by the city hall. I've just gotten off the phone now and explained this succinct Alzheimer's detail that you failed to tell us for far too long and they have waved the claim. Our lawyer had to beg for our forgiveness. If –'

Derisive Deirdre interrupts with venom on her viper tongue. 'No *ifs*, Tim. We *won't* be put in that situation again. He's too much of a liability.'

Dympna says to me, 'It's true. You are a danger to society, Mick. Take our advice and...'

'Disappear from society?' I ask acerbically. 'I feel like I'm a prisoner to my disease.' I turn to Tim; the only one in this room to whom I can relate to. 'Where are the human resources, Tim?' I call out to the HR people. 'You're the Human Resource Department, but you're not giving me any *resources* and I *am* human.'

Long cuts in. 'You can come and visit your elephant any time you want, Mick. We have an open-door policy on that for you.'

'Maybe we should rename that policy?' opines Dympna with a smirk.

HR Deirdre adds, 'Free-of-charge...' And she's being sincere, which only makes it worse.

Long looks at her in disgust and leaves the room. He hands me my severance package on his way out. 'I'm sorry, Mick. Time to take care of yourself, my old friend.'

Without making a scene, I also leave the dragons' den.

Flying Goodbyes

I walk back to the hut in a surreal haze, already feeling like a day-visitor.

When I get to the keepers' hut, Smiler looks up from his itinerary. 'Well?'

'They fired me.'

Smiler totally flips. '*What?!* They *can't!* You've got another good five or six years in you, dammit!'

'Apparently, they're not so good. I'm a human without resources.' I'm struggling to hold in my emotions and I cannot bring myself to look at my friend. 'They have given me a generous early retirement deal. That's about the best I can say.' I point to the figure at the bottom of the page, and even Smiler agrees that it's nothing to be sneezed at.

'Y'know what you should do with some of that money?' He doesn't wait for me to ask. 'Book yourself a flight to Copenhagen and fly from there to Edinburgh, just like you had planned with Gloria. I'll help you with the itineraries.' Smiler smiles that heart-warming smile of his, and I can't help myself from lowering my head into his chest and blubbering like a baby.

In other words, Smiler has just advised me to admit defeat without admitting it.

'It's all over, Smiler. It's all over...' I cry like I've never cried before, even at Gloria's funeral, heaving so deep it hurts physically.

One of the keepers comes in behind us and I feel Smiler waving them away.

'Now what?' he asks, holding me.

I'm ashamed to show my fired face. 'Now, it's time to say goodbye to my old friend, Sinbad, at least as his keeper. Management told me I could come and go as I please. Open-door policy.'

'That's what got you into this in the first place,' he jokes as Dympna had done before him. 'Well, that's better again. Now you can see Sinbad, but you won't have to shovel his shit every day. Good deal.'

Smiler is trying to keep the good side out and that's what good friends do, but we're both trying not to look at the elephant-in-the-room here, which isn't an elephant at all – it's Alzheimer's.

I straighten myself up, wipe away the tears, and walk the two hundred meters from the keepers' hut to the elephant enclosure, trying to hold my head high as Long had said, but I'm wilting inside.

A fresh bout of tears come when I lay eyes on my oblivious elephant and realize that it's all over; our four decade friendship has come to an end in the brief life of just a morning. Sinbad is spraying water on himself to the delight of the visitors. He has no idea what has just happened and I choke up, knowing that it will be just as hard to face Sinbad as it was Smiler. Long did say that I can visit Sinbad whenever I please, but it's not the same. I *enjoyed* cleaning out his dung in the morning – that dung solidified our relationship. It stuck us together into something inseparable like a house made of dung in India.

I open the gate to my elephant's enclosure (making double sure to close it). Visitors watch me with as much curiosity as the elephant, but today I *feel* the visitors watching me. They believe that they live in a world very different to me, but now I am one of them and I feel vulnerable. In the space of one morning, my whole world has been sent topsy-turvy.

I cross Sinbad's enclosure and wait in his sleeping-house, safe from the gaze of the public. Just tearing open the Snickers wrapper is enough to turn Sinbad from his water-trough and come inside to join me. With a tear in my eye, I offer the bar of chocolate to my enormous friend. He takes the chocolate bar with his trunk, flaps his ears in delight, and levers the chocolate into his agape jaws. 'This is the last Snickers, big man. The last supper.' I pat his shoulder. 'I'm going to be making some changes, Sinbad...'

Sinbad's chewing on the toffee and nougat. He squints up his eyes in delight. Like I say, it's the little things in life that are the biggest...

'I won't be around so much anymore, Sinbad, but I'll come to visit you every day and I'll be keeping an eye on you. I'll be your guardian angel.'

I climb onto his feeding area and take his leathery, ear-flap in my hand and whisper into his ear: 'I'm *free*, Sinbad. I'm *free*! They've set me *free*. I won't ever again be behind the bars of this old Victorian zoo. I'll be just like you when you were in Phoenix Park last night.'

Of course, I'm telling a white lie; for me the bars are at home. Give me the zoo bars any day of the week. I think I will take Smiler up on his offer to help with an itinerary; I need some distance from my old self.

'And guess what, old man, I'm going to take your wrinkled, grey, old spirit with me.'

Now, I'm not lying to Sinbad. It sounds a little corny, right, Reader? Wrong. Have you ever buried a loved one and promised them (to yourself really) that they would live on in your dreams? That they would live through your eyes? Okay, granted, I'm treating this as if somebody has just died. But it's not far from the truth. *Something* has just died, but I'm not sure what that something is yet.

And now, another absurdity has just come to the fore of my addled brain. I look at the distance between the top of Sinbad's feeder and the lower part of his back, just behind his neck. I visualize myself stretching out and jumping the last foot or so. If I jump high and far enough, I'll easily clear the space of air between the feeder and Sinbad's back.

You see, Reader, I've always had a secret desire to climb aboard Sinbad and feel his power beneath me and to get an elephant's view of the world, if that's possible. I've spent four-decades-and-a-bit looking up at Sinbad (and I do look up to him, Reader), but, boy, would I give anything to ride him around this enclosure (out of the view of the public or any sneaky-snaky spies the zoo may have). Oh, mercy!

Deciding that this may be my last chance to put something in my bucket list before kicking said bucket, I haul myself onto Sinbad's feeder and study the distance once again, also judging the distance to the ground should I slip…

I crouch…and sprint upwards and reach out into the air…

Just as I launch myself onto my elephant, Tim Long, zoo director, strides into the enclosure. I get distracted mid-air and fall three meters without grace and land, thankfully, on Sinbad's hay-pile. I couldn't have landed better, but the embarrassment hurts.

'What the hell!' is all I hear as I land, winding myself, and whooping to catch my breath.

Long trots over to me and bends down to ask me if I'm okay, but more to the point, 'what in the name of *Sweet Jesus* are you doing?' He lends me his hand and pulls me up to my feet.

I'm dizzy and a little disorientated, but that's nothing new. 'I just wanted to go for a ride on Sinbad.' How humbling, Reader. I feel like an eight year-old. 'It's something I've always wanted to do and that was my last chance. Talk about a messy finish.' I try to appear flippant, but my heart is aching. What a way to go, Reader. The closest I can describe it would be serious pining homesickness, only in my case, I'm sick at the thought of going home.

'Mick,' Long says, pulling me to my feet, 'you're making me nervous and I can't sit at my desk, thinking that you're down here about to break your neck on some foolish wish you've had since a kid – you're *not* a kid anymore. C'mon, I'll accompany you to the gate.'

I flash a long, lonesome glance over my shoulder at Sinbad. He's looking at me in an odd way, just standing there as I leave, like a stuffed elephant in a museum. He knows something's up as I turn my back on my elephant and exit his enclosure.

I briefly think about doing the rounds to say my goodbyes to the other keepers, but I change my mind, a little insulted that they couldn't come to me with their concerns instead of going to management. Reader, I must find out who ratted me out to top brass. Smiler might help me there – he'll be my 'man inside'. I feel a little betrayed, Reader. Especially, seeing as I am the longest-running keeper in the establishment.

You have all seen the film scene: I go to my office (hut) and gather my things (thermos flask and uneaten corned-beef sandwiches) and put them into my backpack (not a cardboard box as you've probably seen on the big screen). I put on my trilby and don't bother changing into my civilian clothes. I leave the zoo uniform on in some obscure statement and stuff my clothes into the backpack.

I follow Long to the main gates. Long holds his hand out and I shake it, uttering an apology for the damage caused by my forgetfulness.

'I'm sorry too that it's ended like this, Mick, but you shouldn't have hidden your illness for so long. All of this could've been avoided if you'd just been up front from the beginning.'

'Would it have saved my job if I had told you the day I got the results?'

Long stalls.

'Exactly. At least I got these six months extra.'

'Remember,' Long calls, 'you can visit any time you feel like it. You have my word.'

'Maybe this evening?' I ask.

When Long sees that I'm not joking he deflects my question with a wave.

Home Alone

I leave my Clio in the zoo car-park so I have an excuse to come back later. I take a short-cut home through Phoenix Park. I am officially retired – my forced retirement. I could just sit on the grass under my feet right here and stare at the clouds floating by aimlessly, if I wanted to, but I don't want to. I feel I'm wasting my time, but now I've got all the time in the world. What will I do with the severance money? I'm a man of leisure now. I could go on a trip to those places that Gloria had planned for us to go to. I could do it in her memory – her legacy. Yes, that might be an option. As I saunter across the grass and carelessly eye teenagers wallowing in the rare afternoon sunshine, I can't help thinking about my beautiful elephant. These teenagers think they're the coolest thing in this park, but the coolest thing happened right where they're lying now, just last night. If only they knew. Sinbad looked so *alive*. He had a light in his eyes that I've never seen before and it grew dull once back in the confines of his enclosure.

I get back to my semi-detached. The place is even quieter than normal when I close the front door behind me: the Swedish grandfather clock (dated 1782 and which has been handed down from generation to generation) has stopped because I forgot to wind it. How apt because time *has* stopped for me. I've *never* forgotten to wind the clock; it's a sacred tradition to wind the clock every Sunday evening for the week ahead. With a heavy heart, I add: *Wind the Clock!!* to yet another Post-It and slap it on the fridge with the rest and call myself a *fucking moron* while I'm at it. My daily routine has come down to a fridge that is one giant multi-colour Post-It.

I make a pot of tea, sit down at my kitchen-table, and look out the window at people passing by on the street. I pick up my harmonica and blow a few notes, but it's not helping, just adding to the doleful greyness of today – the first and last day of the rest of my life. I understand now why Smiler was more concerned with Sinbad's escape. He was looking out for my mental well-being rather than my mental health. Smiler had known that retirement would be the nail in my coffin. Smiler had gazed into the future and had known the outcome of this. It wasn't forgetting to lock in Sinbad; it was the consequence of forgetting.

No matter how hard I try, I cannot keep my mind from Sinbad...and *who*, exactly, is his new keeper?

This has just dawned on me, Reader, *who* is Sinbad's new minder?

I should go down there and inform him or her about Sinbad's little nuances and how he likes a Snickers every now and again for health and safety reasons and how he won't drink water if it's too cold and how it bugs him if...

No, best just forget the whole thing and try and get on with my life. The new keeper will find out for him or herself. I don't want to impose.

I finish my tea and surf the net for half an hour that normally becomes an hour of wasted time. I look at Princes Street in Edinburgh in real time, check out the weather should I decide to go, then do the same for Copenhagen. I gaze at anonymous people walking along the streets, having no idea that there's a stranger watching over them. Is there anybody watching over me?

My landline rings, startling the bejesus out of me. I let it ring out because there's nothing left to say, and I know that Smiler's only ringing me to ask me how I am. Today is a day of contemplation. It needs to sink in; I was only sacked an hour ago.

I take the phone off the hook and go play with my miniatures. I'll carve a tiny elephant in Sinbad's name and smoke twenty cigarettes while I'm at it. Sorry, Reader, you haven't caught me at my finest hour.

No, I'll take a nap. Maybe I'll wake up to find that it's

all been just a nightmare.

I wake disorientated.

I've been dreaming of my elephant. We travelled the world together in half an hour: sand, ice, jungle, we saw it all. I love dream-logic, Reader. In my dream, Sinbad roamed the land freely. He looked *sooo* happy as he picked Snickers from Snicker Trees in Phoenix Park.

When I check the time on my old-school Nokia brick (but what a battery, Reader!), I also see six missed calls from Smiler – that's one every five minutes, not counting the landline calls. Maybe he's got some inside information for me. I just know it. He wouldn't ring seven times during half an hour just to see how I'm coping. There's two things I want to know: who ratted me out at the zoo *and* who is Sinbad's new keeper. I decide not to ring him but meet him face-to-face.

I sit tight for another agonizing hour, before I crack…

At six o'clock, I cut back across Phoenix Park to the zoo car-park. I'm hoping to see Smiler and Sinbad, but when I come up to the gate, I'm refused entry by Gerry 'The Berry', the security guard. I've known The Berry for the last decade and he's acting all, well, *odd*.

'Gerry, it's me, Mick. I haven't been gone that long.'

I notice that The Berry is doing his best to ignore me, so I put my face up to the glass of the kiosk window. 'Gerry, let me in for five minutes. I just want to see Sinbad and make sure he's settled in for the night.'

The Berry grows awkward. 'We're closing, Mick. Be good now and go on home. I'm working extra early this evening cos one of my partners is out sick. Think about the long evening and night I have ahead of me with nothing but wild animals to keep me company.'

'My heart goes out to you, but at least you have a job. Anyway, what's that got to do with anything? Closed to the public, yeah, but keepers are normally here an hour longer.'

'Mick, this is how it is: management have told me that you might show up. I can't let you in until tomorrow when management's around. I heard you almost had a nasty accident riding your elephant around the place this morning. Was Paddy Power giving odds on you finishing the race?' The Berry chuckles at his own joke.

See, Reader? Rumours spread around the zoo faster than the howl of the howler monkey.

Feeling like a stranger, I turn and head back to the public car-park to collect my car, ignoring The Berry's remark.

In the car-park, Smiler pops up out of nowhere with a smirk *and* a knowing glint in his eye...the old Smiler seems to be back on duty.

'Why didn't you answer my calls?' he asks, studying my face for cracks of truth.

'I just didn't have the energy to pick up.'

Smiler nods, understanding my plight. 'I wasn't ringing to see how you were – I *know* how you are. You are shit. I was ringing to tell you about the new keeper that they've hired.'

'Huh? Wait, what?' I can't believe what I'm hearing. *'Already?'*

All body language, Smiler gestures that they sit into his car. Once in the car, he switches on the radio. He's paranoid; the man is paranoid.

'You've been watching spy films again, haven't you, Smiler.'

'Well, yes, I have.' Smiler answers like the guilty kid he is. 'Still, you can never be too careful. What I'm about to tell you is of a sensitive nature.'

'Go on...'

'Seems like this new keeper was waiting for you to be escorted off the premises before he jumped in your grave. Apparently, this guy was on a waiting-list and was waiting for one of us to fly the nest. He was just lurking in the shadows like a guy waiting for an organ donor to be involved in some terrible accident.'

'Jesus, Smiler, but you really come out with some dark stuff sometimes. I know you've got marriage problems, but really?'

'By the way,' Smiler adds, 'you know the lion that roars at the beginning of the MGM films? He was born in Dublin zoo. How many years have I been here and I never knew that till this morning.'

'Uh-huh. Have you ever given your child to a stranger, Smiler?'

'What?'

'Maybe you could tell me more about this new keeper? I appreciate the lion trivia, *but...*'

'I heard that he's family to HR Deirdre Higgins. Sitting up there at the top of the pile.'

'We've met,' I add sourly. 'That makes sense; she seemed to be in a hurry to get me off the premises.'

'Word on the grapevine is that he's an unemployed security-guard who kept a couple of guinea-pigs named George and Mildred when he was a child, but that's about it as far as animal management is concerned.'

Now, I have no doubt in my mind. 'She was gunning for me to be off the premises ASAP. She used the excuse of Sinbad's escape to get me out.'

Smiler looks at me. 'Yes, that minor detail of the rampaging elephant probably did influence her decision. Anyway, Guinea-Pig starts tomorrow.'

'What?!'

'Mick, calm the fuck down, please. If I were you, I'd avail of Long's open invitation and make sure you show up here tomorrow to give our new friend some friendly advice on how to look after animals. In the mean time, I'm going to keep an eye on this mysterious cuckoo.' Smiler lowers the radio and pulls on his seat-belt.

'Good, good. One more thing…'

'Lay it on me, baby. Anything for Mick.'

'Any idea who ratted me out to management?'

Smiler shakes his head, raises radio volume once again, and treats the question as if it should be forgotten.

I take that as a *No* and get out of the car.

'Did you ever think that they might've been trying to help you?' Smiler asks/tells me through his open window as he moves off.

'By telling HR that I screwed up?' I call back. 'Who needs that kind of help, Smiler?'

He sticks his hand out the window and points at me. 'We love you, man. Look at it from our point of view. You'll find out in due course, I'm sure.'

Why is Smiler backing up the snake in the grass? 'Sorry, it's not my finest moment...It just seems that the world is out to get me.'

Smiler understands. '"I hear you" as my grandson says.' He drives off.

I wave to Smiler for the inside info and get into my old Clio, but not without looking over my shoulder at the closing zoo gates and my best friend beyond and out of sight. It physically hurts to drive off, but I've no choice. It must be like severing yourself from your child on the first day of school.

Back at home, I once again become obsessed with the little things in life. I try to find a house routine. I had something good going for the hours between after-work and bed-time, but now I've got the whole day to kill. Routine: it is so important, Reader, it's the anchor that anchors our day. Without an anchor we wander at sea. Now that's about as philosophical as I'm going to get, so I'll bid you good night.

The New Keeper

The following morning, I'm standing at the zoo gates at nine sharp. It's odd standing in the queue. In a stranger way, I feel that I've *never* worked at the zoo and if I have, it's merely a hazy memory. I feel excited to see my elephant, but I can't help thinking that I must look pretty pathetic to my ex-colleagues – a little simple, even.

The Berry happily waves me through, unlike yesterday, informing me that today there's top brass milling around as if I'm still working here and to make sure I look busy.

I thank The Berry for the useless information and make for the elephant enclosure with my heart pounding and clammy-hand syndrome setting in. Anybody would think that I was going to meet my long-lost family at an airport gate. The only thing that would top this right now is if I was going to meet my Glow. I'd give anything for a cigarette.

Reader, sometimes, I have nightmares where she is alive again; it doesn't become the nightmare until I wake. Sorry about that sudden dip in proceedings; these bouts of melancholy creep on me at any time of the day. By the way, while we're on the subject, I went to the "dark side" last night, as Smiler calls it. I went online to check prices to Edinburgh and Copenhagen, but I ended up looking at old photographs of Gloria and myself. It's not good for the head, so I'll say no more about the subject.

I walk down the main thoroughfare. I don't want to engage in conversation with the other keepers until I find out who has been telling tales to HR about me, plus I don't feel part of their world anymore. When I have put some distance between the zoo and me, then I'd like to have a chat with a select few keepers, but until then, it just seems too strange and ultimately sad.

I casually saunter up to the elephant enclosure, trying to be nonchalant about the whole thing when what I really want to do is make a crazy run for it, yelling: 'Sinbad! Elephant!' Brutal, basic, and honest.

But screaming unrequited love for my elephant isn't conducive to my little plan that I've got here this morning. I decide that I prefer to see how this new keeper works without introducing myself first; that gives me the upper hand. I'll mingle with the visitors.

I peer into the enclosure through a bunch of tourists of Asian extraction, clicking their expensive cameras at anything that moves (and doesn't move) and see the new keeper for the first time...

And first impressions last, Reader...

Sinbad is standing on the new keeper's shovel (my old shovel) and, if my eyes aren't deceiving me, the keeper is attempting to shove my elephant, heaving on his rump, Reader, to get him off the shovel. The tourists are really lapping up this zoo/circus tragi-comedy; it *would* be a comedy if it wasn't so tragic.

I begin to panic...

To my addled mind, all I see is a sea of foreign slanted eyes, straight black hair, and laughing, gaping mouths. It's the same face over and over again. They are in stitches, virtually falling in over the wall to get the snap they will later put up on that thing they call Facebook. I don't know if I'm being politically correct or incorrect and if it's politically correct to even mention being politically correct, but I'm calling it like I see it, dammit, and it's making me *angry* – not the Asian tourists (they could be from Mars for all I care), but how my unwitting elephant has been degraded to a show for cheap laughs. Oh mercy, I can't think straight.

The red-faced keeper punches his own head before turning his wrath on Sinbad. I can't believe what I'm seeing. He may as well be punching at the sky – Sinbad doesn't even know he's there.

We know he's there, though. Fucking moron!

A hush descends among the tourists...they're not clicking anymore...

One little girl is though, I notice. She's got one of those disposable cardboard cameras and she's clicking and whirring like there's no tomorrow: *click ... wind ... click ...wind...*

The oblivious keeper's demeanour suddenly changes to rage and we all see how he reaches for the pitch-fork only to discover that he's got a horrified audience looking at him from the other side of the glass. I want to tell management what I've just witnessed, but they'll think that I'm just trying to paint the 'keeper' in their bad books, so I can move back in. I need a witness, I've got them standing all around me, but I'm not up for a conversation with one of them. Then I see the little girl, taking snaps of her shoes now.

Desperate for evidence, I approach her.

The parents intercept.

'I need the camera...' No time for introductions...

I know, just by the way they are looking at me, that the parents don't understand and the little girl, even less. So, I repeat myself, slowly and loudly, for the hard of hearing: *'I...neeed...theee...caaameraaa...'*

'We understand you perfectly,' says the mother in English better than mine, 'but we don't understand *why* you need our daughter's camera...'

Fair question. I quickly explain who I am and what I've just seen – what we have *all* just seen – and how their daughter has captured everything on her cardboard camera. 'Do it for the elephant!' I finally plead, then hand them twenty euro...sugar-coating it with another tenner when I see them begin to think.

Not being stupid and being animal-lovers, they hand over the camera. The little girl's bottom lip drops before she finally breaks out in a screaming cry, but the parents explain in a language foreign to me. She looks up at me with big, teary eyes and nods. We exchange camera and money, but importantly, an understanding. Maybe I'm the foreign one, after all.

I leave the enclosure and storm down to HR where I meet my ex-boss Tim Long in the hallway.

'We couldn't keep you away for long,' he jokes. 'Here on work experience?'

In anger, I hand over the camera to him. 'Look!'

'Um, there's a Lost and Found at the gate entrance, Mick, you know that.'

I'm livid. I can hardly construct words in my mouth. 'I've just witnessed – along with a Japanese or Korean or Chinese tour – your new "keeper" punch my elephant and reach for the pitch-fork before he realized that people were watching…I have it all here on camera. Tim, he was trying to push the elephant off his shovel that was lying on the ground. That's what we're dealing with here.'

Long sighs. 'Okay, I'll look into it.'

'I know what you're doing. Don't try to fob me off, Tim. You're going to have trouble with that guy. I've just seen him for the first time, and I can already tell you that he needs anger management classes. I don't want my elephant to be his punch-bag. And don't think that I'm trying to weasel my way back in here. I've taken on board what you said and I think it's a good time to leave and concentrate on other things.' I'm not fully convinced of what I'm telling Long, but I have come around to his way of thinking, a little. Maybe it is time to face my forgetting illness and make provisions for the future. That severance package would go a long way in an old folks' home, oh mercy.

'Develop the photos and you'll see for yourself…'

Long smiles at me and holds my shoulders. 'I'll go into my dark-room right now and develop this.'

'Don't patronize me, Tim. We're both too long in the

tooth for that.'

'I told you that I'll look into it. Now, if you'll excuse me, I have to go to a meeting and speak to people higher than me, *and* the insurance sharks, about how you let an elephant roam free in Dublin. The last time I had to deal with this lot was when that Jehovah's Witness jumped into the big cat enclosure expecting to be at one with nature.'

There's no more to be said here so I leave. I try to will myself from straying back to the elephant enclosure, but I give in, and watch the circus act once again. It's a one-clown circus and the keeper's still trying to get Sinbad to stand off the shovel. But Sinbad is happy munching on his hay and oblivious to Coco the clown hammering at his rump. I let the new keeper suffer a little more for the benefit of the tourists and me, but then I put him out of his misery. I go outside and call over to him: 'Sinbad, over here.'

The elephant immediately reacts to my voice. I wave a Snickers and start to unwrap it. Sinbad flaps his ears and makes a sudden dive to our wall, leaving the visitors *oohing* and *aahing* and snapping selfies with uncertain smiles as the elephant looms into frame behind them.

Sinbad skids to a stop and uncurls his trunk into the group to seek out the Snickers. The tourists are loving it as his trunk slides in and out of their clothes and ruffles their hair in search of chocolate. I give Sinbad the chocolate bar and he taps my head in his own special way of saying *hello*. It brings a tear to my eye. I spot the little girl in the crowd that has gathered along the fence and give her another Snickers and tell her to give it to my elephant. She does so with trepidation. She beams as Sinbad plucks it from her open palm. I hope this memory will last a lot longer than a photograph will.

Meanwhile, the keeper, beetroot-red, picks up his warped shovel and approaches me. 'Dr. Doolittle, I presume?' the keeper says, holding out his hand in a not-too-enthusiastic manner.

I accept his limp hand-shake and introduce myself. I'm already rankled by his insipid nature. I notice he's got a tattoo that runs the length of his forearm which reads: *Made in China* in that homogeneous text that the expression is normally written in. I don't believe he was made in China, but I do believe he is disposable.

The keeper tells me that his name is 'Bean', which is a nickname, then jokingly tells me that he won't tell me his real name until he "knows me a little better". Whatever *that* means…not that he'll ever "know me a little better" and not that I really want to know.

I quickly come to the conclusion, Reader, that I don't care all that much for Bean. Okay, I'll keep an open mind about his working practice, but as a person, I'll skip dessert, thanks.

Meanwhile, Sinbad is all over me. He's missed me.

'Would you mind if I come in and spend a little time with Sinbad?'

Bean hesitates. 'That's probably not such a good idea.'

'Oh?'

'In my head,' pointing to his temples with both forefingers, as if I didn't know where his head was (I think it's up his arse, but that's beside the point), 'I was thinking that it would be a *greeeat* idea, but my aunt told me that you might make the occasional call to say hello to the elephant. We can't let you in the actual enclosure…'

'*We?!*'

'…for insurance purposes…' reaming it off, probably drilled into him by his poisonous aunt. 'However, you can watch him all day from the side-lines if that suits you – but as a visitor.'

I feel betrayed. Already, I've been reduced to the status of visitor after decades of working in the zoo. It makes me sick to hear this young guinea-pig babysitter lay down the law to me, to *me* who gave most of my life to the zoo. It's just so frustrating to see Sinbad, but not being able to be with him. I'd love to give him a hug right now, but I'm too angry and leave the enclosure, telling the new upstart to keep an eye on his shovel and a closer eye on his pitch-fork.

I pop my head into the keeper's hut and see that it's full of keepers on break. Nothing has changed, as if I never stopped working here. Without wanting to be noticed and having to answer questions, I ease the door shut behind me and cross to the public car-park and drive off.

As I make my way home, my eyes momentarily drop to my right hand on the gear-stick and I remember when Gloria and I were so in love that she changed gears for me. We were inseparable, as inseparable as me and my elephant. Only now, Sinbad's been taken from me too. In a way, and I know you'll hate me for saying this, Reader, but in a way, I prefer my Glow's death because death is final and I don't have to share her with anybody. I *do* have to share Sinbad – with a fucking moron.

I feel home-sick again: sick of being at home.

The Attack

For the next fortnight, passing from February into March, I visit my fond, old friend every day. I stand in the queue at the zoo gates nine a.m. sharp, like a loyal dog waiting for its master. The ticket people wave me through the zoo stalls each morning with a friendly smile. In a way, I feel like I'm still working at the zoo...in another way, I feel a little stupid.

I watch my elephant from behind the thick pane of glass or sometimes go outside and sit by his wall. But, he doesn't come out as much as he used to. I'm under the strong suspicion that Sinbad seems a little down. I'm not sure if that's just me, but he's a little too static for my liking. During these two weeks, Sinbad seems to sink further into this lethargy that I don't like very much. I feel helpless. All I want to do is crank up Ravi Shankar and sit by him, pass him a Snickers, and wonder what he's thinking. But Bean doesn't let me near him. He makes life difficult for me.

Reader, if you ever happen to be a new mom or dad looking through hospital glass at your new baby, then I imagine you'll know how I feel these days. Or better again, sitting in a prison's visitor room with a pane of glass between you and your loved one.

There's a longing there that I can barely describe or live with because, Reader, I realize now that Sinbad is my only connection to my life as Mick Munroe; when he goes I'll be wandering at sea – far out at sea when the Alzheimer's finally robs me of who I am. I'm desperate, in other words. Sorry, Reader, I don't mean to complain, but you're all I've got. Hmm? Talk to Smiler? Smiler's too busy working out his itineraries to patch things up with his wife, Kelly.

By Wednesday, Sinbad doesn't even want to go outside in the sunshine; just stares at his wall like a mental patient.

'Sinbad!' I call out to him on impulse, but he can't hear

me from this side of the reinforced glass – the visitors hear me though…I'm letting my emotions get the better of me, which is never a good thing.

On Thursday, Sinbad's got all the signs of depression. I can't stand behind these bars and watch my old friend sink into oblivion…If he happened to look through his bars he would see his depressed best friend looking back at him through his bars in a mirror-effect.

On Friday, I decide to call into the monkey-house to see Smiler and ask if he has any inside information. He tells me, while making a fruit cocktail for his orang-utans, that the other keepers don't like the new keeper, Bean, because he's a tell-tale and mentions every little detail to Devil Deirdre in HR. 'He's a sneak and should be in the reptile house,' sums up Smiler.

I tell Smiler to keep an eye on Sinbad for me. 'Promise?'

'Promise. Now, will you please *fuck off* and let me get on with my monkey work.'

I huff a tired chuckle, as does Smiler.

I go home for the day and dedicate myself to my miniatures once again, people-gaze on the Edinburgh webcam (I can see Glow and myself walking along Princes Street with shopping bags), play the harmonica, mess around with my clocks, and generally wither. Though I do write daily in my diary – it's what you are reading now, Reader. This diary keeps me afloat because, like I said, it's good to talk. However, I don't know if Bob Hoskins includes "talking to yourself" in his famous expression. My diary is in fact my memory book. I'm writing down every little thing I do, so that when the time comes, I can read how Mick Munroe was and try to emulate him. I will try to stay true to me: it's more than a diary – it's a book called 'Me'.

There are some of you out there with experience with Alzheimer's and you're saying to yourself: *this guy's wasting his time – when your head goes, your head goes…poof!*

Okay, fair enough, but how about humouring me? It's helping me get through this. It just might get me through the later stages. I know I probably won't be able to read these words at the end, but by then, who cares? Right? I want to remember who I am for as long as I can.

On Saturday morning, Smiler's at the ticket office to meet me, knowing that I'd be visiting my friend. Something's up – Smiler is never here at this time of the morning and I can see his dour expression as I cross the car-park. He's normally busy with his monkeys. He comes up to meet me, just as I come through the turn-style. He stands in my path and starts giving me some itinerary ideas for my proposed Copenhagen-Edinburgh trip.

'I've known you long enough,' I say to Smiler, 'to know that there's something up, now will you *stop* treating me like a kid. What's wrong? It's obvious you're trying to divert me.'

Smiler decides to take the *Huh?* approach. 'What do you mean?'

'It's nine o'clock in the morning. You're always with your monkeys at this time. You're a stickler for routine just as much as I am.' I glance over my shoulder. 'What's *wrong?*' I suddenly feel the flutter of nerves that comes with bad news. My insides surge.

Smiler grows shifty and leads me discreetly by the arm to the Coke machine that is full of fizzy drink cans waiting to explode in visitors' faces, but still out-of-stock in Fanta and Lilt, I notice.

For a moment, I think that Smiler's going to tell me that his money has gotten stuck in the machine and ask me for a coin, but he uses the machine as a diversion. He's paranoid again. With cautious glances, Smiler warns me from the side of his mouth. 'Don't go down there…'

'Why?'

Smiler's visibly upset. 'Just turn around and go home, then sit tight and wait for me to call you.'

'*Smiler!?*'

Smiler panics for the first time in his life and pops a euro in the Coke machine and presses the Fanta button. He's taking his role as spy very seriously, but curses under his breath when he sees that the machine is out of Fanta, so opts for Lilt and curses again. Finally, he kicks the machine and chooses Coke. 'It's Sinbad.'

I feel the blood drain from face. 'I had gotten that far in my head...' My lips have turned dry.

'He was, um, injured.' Smiler pops his can open and is sprayed all over his overalls and new work-boots. He curses and I almost utter an apology. I didn't think cans could hold fizz for so long. Feeling as if I'm living a déjà vu, I ask, 'Can you be more specific?'

Smiler takes a gulp of Coke and the fizz comes down his nose and he's a jittering mass of mess. 'Stabbed with a pitch-fork...'

I grow woozy. Pins and needles tingle in my fingers and I know I'm about to pass out. I flop to the wet concrete and my trilby rolls off my head. I sit there in a dazed state for what seems a century.

Smiler grabs me and drags me up to my feet and hands me back my trilby. 'Pull yourself together, man.'

The second my head clears, I make a break for Sinbad's enclosure...

Smiler wrestles me into a corner. I'm frantic, not sure whether I want to run screaming and never come back or run screaming towards Sinbad. The last thing I want to do is listen to Smiler. 'Get the fuck off me!'

'Listen...*Listen!* This is how it is. One of the keepers spotted four puncture marks in your elephant's rump. Top brass are down there now with the vets and the rest of the crew, insurance company, the whole shebang. There's going to be an inquiry.'

I shake my head and look at the ground. 'I knew it; I *knew* it when I saw him. Fucking moron! He's the kind of guy that should be hidden in the back of a warehouse somewhere so the public shouldn't have to deal with him. Get him counting cardboard boxes…'

'But there's no evidence that he did it.'

'Oh, c'mon, are you trying to tell me that he sat on a pitch-fork, Smiler?!'

'That's Bean's story and he's sticking to it.'

'What?!' I can't take it anymore. 'I can't stand by and watch this happen, Smiler.' I struggle in Smiler's grip, but he's got me in some kind of wrestle tackle and I wouldn't be surprised if Smiler has taken up wrestling night classes, just to get away from the wife. 'I love that goddamn elephant! C'mon, you should understand that! You sleep with your monkeys when you're in the dog-house with Kelly.'

Smiler grits his teeth. 'I told you never to bring that up, especially here.' He gulps a deep breath of fresh air. 'Look, getting involved is not going to make matters any better. You're letting your emotions get in the way, Mick – you always did, if you don't mind my saying so. Go home and wait for me to call you. Let me be your eyes. I'm the ghost and I'll haunt the bastard until I find the truth – call me Slimer.'

We both smile at that one.

I already regret saying: 'You weren't watching when he stabbed my elephant…'

'Mick, I know how you feel. If I was in your boots, I'd feel so *fucking* angry, but it's completely useless anger. Go home and do something to get your mind off the zoo.'

'Who do you think informed Long about Sinbad's wound?'

Smiler nods and thumbs his chest.

'Thanks.'

'It could've gone unnoticed. I'm sorry I wasn't there to stop the bastard, but what would the chances be of being there in the moment?'

'Okay, sorry. I take back what I said. You've a job to do as well.'

'I'm watching him, Mick. But you need to listen to me. I don't want you going down there now because that's not going to help anything. You're just going to go nuts and complicate things.'

'I *need* to see him, Smiler.'

'Not now, don't get involved. You don't work here anymore. I know that's hard to hear, but those are the cold facts. Play it cool and we'll win in the end.' Smiler squeezes my shoulders and stares me in the eyes. 'You are number one now. If you need anything, let me know. Take a hike…'

We both know he's talking about my illness. Everything is swallowing me up! 'No!' I yell and make a run for it, but Smiler pins me to the wall. 'I'm *telling* you as your friend that you're not fucking *working* at the zoo anymore. You cannot go and see your elephant today. Let it go, Mick.'

I take Smiler's hands off me and dig in my pocket for some loose change, count it, and hold it up to him. 'I'm a paying punter and I'm paying to visit the zoo.'

Smiler shakes his head and waves his hands. 'I'm out.' He heads back the way he had come.

I double back and make my way to the ticket kiosk and pay my fare (even though I have already been inside the zoo and Smiler's gone), but Janice, the ticket-lady, pushes my ball of change back to me. 'Your money is no good here, Mick.'

I take a deep breath and try to smile. 'Does that mean my money isn't valid currency or you're letting me pass without paying?'

She waves me through and I stuff the ball of change back into my pocket.

Gerry the Berry, the security guard, nods me through, though reluctantly. 'I never saw you,' I hear The Berry's voice call as I pass through the turn-style once again. At the same time, Janice says with a wink: 'Go and take care of your elephant.'

I trot-walk down past the reptile house, nod a brief salute to the majestic flamingos foraging at the lakeside, and arrive at the elephant enclosure. Visitors have gathered around to see what all the commotion is. The enclosure is cordoned off with yellow tape as if it were a crime-scene – and it is, Reader, as far as I'm concerned.

Almost in tears, and *trying* to control my surging anger, I duck under the tape and slip inside Sinbad's house…

My breath is taken from me…

Sinbad is *swaying* because he cannot stand up straight. He's holding his left hind leg off the ground. I see Bean flippantly explaining what happened to Long along with more HR. Interesting to note that his high-power aunt is nowhere to be seen.

What I decide to do next, Reader, might shock you…I know it shocks me. There's only one way to deal with a bully and that's to…

I sprint into Sinbad's living-space and dive head-long into Bean's mid-riff, lifting him off the ground, pushing him back two meters in the air, winding him, then pummelling him onto the floor. I pin him to the ground. My intention isn't to beat Bean because I'm not that kind of ex-keeper, but to interrogate him and scare the truth out of him…

But I don't get a chance. Long and the police are pulling me off the slime-ball.

'Who is this??' calls one of the police, as he leaps onto my back and tries to get a hold of my wrists. But I won't let him. It's just me and this sadistic Made in China fucker.

'Why did you do it?! Sinbad is a gentle giant! Fucking moron!!'

'He's okay!' Long shouts, not sure whether to pull the policeman off me, punch me, or let me at Bean. 'He's the old elephant keeper! Let him go!'

Then I feel another pair of hands behind me. They try to pull me off Bean, but I'm crazy and have the strength of a madman. *'Get off me!! This prick needs to answer for his crime, and this is the only way this kind of moron understands!'*

Suddenly, I realize that it isn't an extra pair of hands behind me, but a trunk grappling for my attention.

I freeze and look over my shoulder to see Sinbad towering over me. I don't know if Sinbad is trying to defend me, call me off, or simply looking for a Snickers.

The fight seeps out of me. Seeing my elephant step in as I fight for his honour saps me of my energy and my madman strength fizzles away. I collapse in an exhausted heap next to my enemy, looking up into Sinbad's teary eyes.

The others pull me off Bean.

I get to my feet, panting and red-faced, adrenaline running through my system. I can barely stand with the jitters.

I've never seen Long so angry. 'Go home!' He yells at me like I'm a dog that has strayed into the zoo. *'Home!!'*

I don't move. 'Not until you fire this excuse for a keeper. He should be working in a slaughterhouse!'

'I suggest you take his advice and leave,' answers the policewoman. 'We could book you for a number of offences already.'

Long pleads with me with his eyes.

'I'll be back,' I warn, as Arnold Schwarzenegger has done before me, and stomp out of the premises, but not without voicing my opinion. 'Tim, fire that evil bastard before he kills Sinbad. If you don't do it for the elephant, then do it for the sales that you'll lose when he's gone because they *all* come to see Sinbad.' It's true and Long knows it. Sinbad is a famous elephant at the zoo, being the oldest elephant in the country and one of the oldest in Europe.

'I'm gonna sue you!' cries Bean.

'Fucking moron!' I yell back, quoting my favourite insult. I'm not worried about the moron's idle threat. 'Your head should be used to open locked doors!' I don't know where this comes from, but I like it.

I'd be lying to you, Reader, if I said that I didn't shed a tear on the journey home, thinking about my helpless friend, trapped in a torture chamber. A little dramatic? Maybe, but that's just how I feel right now.

I spend the longest weekend of my life at home. On Sunday I get into my Clio several times to head down to the zoo and find out what the hell is going on, but several times I just sit there in my driveway, staring at everything, asking myself if I should go to see my elephant or "sit tight" as Smiler had suggested. Smiler hasn't called me, so I call Smiler, but I forgot that he switches off his phone at the weekend. I could go around to his place which is just a few streets from me, but I don't want to intrude, even though he did give me an open invite to visit. I'm not sure how things are between Kelly and himself.

So, I "sit tight".

Enough is Enough

I finally make it to Monday morning, but only just about. Somehow, I struggle through Monday and at a minute to 6pm in the evening I finally crack…

I jump into the Clio. This time I don't just sit in and stare at the front wall of my house (which needs a paint). I rev it up and drive down to the zoo, driving double the speed limit, and almost killing a lollipop lady and destroying her lollipop, already having set an impending disaster in my exhausted mind.

I park up in the zoo car-park and will myself to stay here. After a short wait, listening to Ravi Shankar on my CD player (I take a CD player around in the back-seat because my Clio barely has a radio), Smiler appears at the zoo gates after a long day with the monkeys, looking even more monkey than usual. Today is one of those days, practically dragging himself across the car-park on his knuckles. Maybe it's a good moment to invite him to a pint in our local.

'Smiler.' I pop up amongst the cars in the car-park, startling him.

'Munroe, fancy seeing you here.'

'Do you have any more information for me?'

'Regarding?' Smiler is in one of his lazy, sarcastic moods.

'Regarding a four-tonne Indian elephant.'

'Your elephant is fine. He's being treated by the zoo vets as we speak. I just took a run down there to sniff it out. Sinbad's on his own and they're changing his bandages, sterilizing, vet-stuff, etc.'

I can't believe I'm even having this conversation. I don't know why, but I'm getting the impression that Smiler's hiding something from me. 'And Bean? He's kicked the bucket, right?' I feel a cold sweat coming on….

Smiler hesitates.

'*Right?*'

'They gave him a warning and put it down to inexperience.'

Red-hot panic rises inside me all over again. '*A written warning?!* If I go out and stab somebody on the street with a table fork, d'ya think the judge'll put that down to *inexperience?!* "Next time, use a pitch-fork, son." Is that what the judge'll say?? My arse, he will!'

And just to rub it in, Smiler tells me: 'It wasn't even a written warning; more of a slap on the wrist.'

There's something else. I just *know* it. 'Fancy a pint?' If there's any way to Smiler's heart then it's through a pint of creamy Guinness.

Smiler answers without hesitation, 'I'll drive.'

We cross the car-park and get into Smiler's beat-up Ford Focus. We crawl through Dublin's rush-hour traffic where nobody's in any rush. It takes us twenty minutes to travel a mile to our local, *Sod a' Turf*, or simply *The Sod* to you, Reader.

As is custom, the smell of peat turf is thick on the air when we go inside. It's an old-school pub, just how I like 'em, and Chops Doswell maintains the pub as it was maintained a century ago. Fixtures and fittings are coated in a sticky smoke resin that has built up over the years. All the usual suspects are perched at the low-lit bar. They flash Smiler and I subliminal salutes. Chops is behind the wide counter, making himself look busy while staring at his reflection in the wall-mirror behind the 80's cash-till, tending to his side-chops with a comb. One of the drinkers – a Santa Claus look-alike – is playing the spoons to anybody who will listen.

'You look beautiful this evening,' says Smiler, 'but any chance of getting two pints of stout? Elvis left the building long ago.'

Chops' side-chops are immaculate as always and he

greets us with that stern, dried-up, furrowed gaze that forty-cigarettes-a-day plus pre-ban secondary smoke has lent him.

Rashers Raleigh briefly takes his gaze from the horse-racing on the flat-screen TV (I hate TVs in bars, Reader) and looks at me. 'I hear you hung up your pitch-fork, Mick? Is that true? I thought you'd see it out to the bitter end.'

The pitch-fork wasn't hung up, but I know who I'd like to hang up. 'I *did* see it out to the bitter end.' Rashers means working till retirement age of 65, but I'm not in any mood for light banter, especially any mention of a pitch-fork. Besides, I don't want to get into the reason why I've retired. So, I confirm the rumours (playing with words a little) and take myself to the snug, which is a private little corner of the pub, sectioned off from the rest by stain-glass; *The Snug* is stencilled into the stain-glass in golden Celtic font.

Smiler sits in beside me and places two creamy pints of Guinness on the table.

I sink half the Guinness in two gulps and surprise myself by beginning to cry... The pressure of the last few days finally gets to me: being fired ... Sinbad ... Alzheimer's ... Glow...

Smiler, as if waiting for this, puts his arm around my shoulder and gives a brief squeeze. 'The Guinness isn't that bad,' he jokes, trying to lighten the tension in the snug because it's anything but snug now. It's about as close as two heterosexual men can get in the snug, but I can't help the tears that come up from deep inside the well.

We just sit there and drink our pints in silence while I *scream-cry* into the dark Guinness, making it look like I'm drinking it. I have to say, Reader, it feels *so* good to have a cry now and again – the release is better than any drug.

'C'mon,' Smiler coaxes me, 'it's not that bad.'

'Yes it is. I'm lonely, depressed, and right now, I don't

see that there's much to live for.'

'Don't talk rubbish,' sums up Smiler's advice, but stops when he sees the haunted look in my eyes. He takes that as his cue to call two more pints.

'I'm scared, Smiler.'

Behind us, some intoxicated drinker kicks into a heartfelt rendition of *Kumbaya My Lord...*

'I can't sleep and I constantly dream of Sinbad – sometimes good, other times bad. The good dreams are always the same: Sinbad is roaming free in the countryside. The bad dreams – the nightmares – are always the same too: Sinbad is...' I can't get it out, so I drink my pint.

Smiler clears his throat and brings up a new itinerary. He produces leaflets and maps and lays them out on the table. Then Smiler produces his magnifying glass to add to the mystique. 'The wife and myself are thinking of going to Rome for a long weekend to *re-light the fire...*' He attempts to sing these last few words before zooming in with his magnifying tool and pointing to the centre of the city on the map. 'There's a little known area right in the centre of Rome that tourists rarely visit.' His finger is tapping Vatican City, as far as I can see. Maybe Smiler's hidden location is a few streets away, but his stubby forefinger is definitely on St. Peter's Square. 'I'll do some detective work and see if I can find a local guide willing to get us there – a priest or something.' He fails to tell me what or where it is.

Smiler knocks back his second pint in uncharacteristically dramatic fashion, folds away his itinerary in crisp fashion, and gets up to leave. 'You stay and enjoy your pint. I have to clean out the gutters. You okay to walk home? You're just around the corner...'

I nod, but I'm a little confused. Before I know it, Smiler has left the premises, scratching his behind as he exits the door. All that scratching is going to get him into trouble some day. Before he shuts the door behind him, Smiler looks back and tells me that Gerry The Berry is on night duty and goes for his version of breakfast at midnight. 'He crosses over to that 24-hour Chinese. He shouldn't leave the zoo grounds; he *should* eat in the hut, but who cares?'

Bizarre. What's odder is that it is pitch dark outside – who cleans gutters in the dark, Reader? And another thing: I *know* The Berry's routine; he's been going to the same Chinese restaurant since I can remember despite the triple-heart bypass.

Slightly startled at Smiler's behaviour, I do as he says and sip my pint, listening to the commentary of the horse-racing and the intermittent low mumble of pub banter behind me. My thoughts wander back to my elephant, as always. Without wanting to torture myself any further, I quickly finish my drink and lay the glass on the table in front of me.

Then I see them…

Reader, there's a set of shiny keys on the sofa beside me…

I pick up the keys and run to the door. On the street outside, Smiler's nowhere to be seen under the streetlights, so I go back inside and, being snug in the snug, I order one more pint for the road, which is one more than my usual two and I shouldn't really, but now I'm a man of leisure.

Chops delivers the fresh pint and sees me gazing at the newly-cut keys in my hand.

'That's a new one,' Chops observes, in his smoky tones, 'normally people forget where they left their keys, but you look as if you've forgotten which door the keys open,' his moving lips hardly visible beneath his smoke-stained moustache.

I half-heartedly laugh off Chops' comment – *half-*heartedly because it's not too far from the truth these days. We won't go there, Reader.

Chops floats away…but something else comes to the fore now: I'm beginning to think that Smiler left these keys

67

on purpose. What was it he had said before he left?

Something about The Berry going for breakfast at midnight. Now, that's beginning to make sense, too.

Is my mind playing tricks with me?

I sup a little more and suddenly, I realize what I'm holding: *zoo* keys! Oh, mercy!

If I'm not mistaken, Smiler has left this fresh set of keys for me to go and have a little sneak into see Sinbad. He conveniently forgot these keys because then he wasn't guilty of anything and why would he give me the useless information that the security guard breaks off for breakfast at midnight? It all makes perfect sense. And cleaning the gutters? C'mon, Smiler, is that the best you can do?

I turn to get a look at the Heineken clock over the bar. I see that it's just after ten pm – another two hours before The Berry goes for midnight breakfast.

Will I dare, Reader? Do I have much to lose? You know those times when you know that you've already made up your mind about doing something, but you just haven't faced up to it yet? The gentle warm buzz of the three pints of Guinness has been replaced by adrenaline.

I'm going to do it, Reader! I decide to take my life in my hands and make that visit to my dear, old friend. It's all about the elephant. Consequences don't have consequence for me anymore.

I take a short-cut home and watch through the TV until eleven p.m. That's when my heart starts to beat a little faster and I begin to yawn, not because it's my bed-time, but because I'm nervous – nervous about breaking into Dublin Zoo.

The Great Escape

It's a windy night. The leaves rustle in the trees above me and the swaying branches cast shadows along the pavement. Thankfully the rain has held off until now. By 11:30pm, I'm pacing the green spiked fence that runs along the perimeter of the zoo. I decided at the last minute to leave the car behind. I didn't bring the Clio because it would be spotted and any zoo staff would know my car straight away.

I feel alive, Reader! My head is clearer than it has been in months, but I have to admit that the gravity of the situation doesn't have any, well, gravity: I'm floating around the perimeter of the zoo tonight, like a suspicious ghost up to no good. I'm dizzy at the prospects of what this crazy night will bring. Something big is coming…Something that will have consequences, but I'm not sure what those consequences are, nor do I really care –

Shush!

There goes Gerry The Berry right on schedule, just as Smiler had said, crossing the street to the Chinese restaurant with seventy-two stitches criss-crossing his chest following his triple by-pass. What a dolt.

I wait a few minutes to make sure The Berry doesn't decide to get a spring-roll take-away at the last minute, then casually saunter up to the gates and perform a quick reconnaissance after pulling my anorak high over my face and lowering my trilby. As I pass by the locked gates, I see that the little security hut is completely empty. What would the precious HR department say if they saw that? Devil Deirdre and Dympna Spawn… Too late, I'm about to spill the beans on that one. No offence, Berry, but I'm walking on a higher plain now.

I take out the keys Smiler had left for me and go to put them in the gate-lock, but I grow fidgety. I try to stay cool, but I'm not cool by nature, and I crumble into a nervous bowl of jelly. I try again, this time the key slips into the main gate's lock.

Click…

'I knew it!' I rejoice, quickly checking myself.

I've just got the key into the lock when I hear a noise behind me. My natural defences tell me to lock the gate and pull out the key. I do so with numb fingers, then bend down to tie my non-existent shoelaces on my leatherette slip-ons. Then, from the corner of my eye, I see what was making the noise: a pizza box blowing along the street…

So I try again.

I twist the key…

I almost lose control of my shaking hands when the gate clicks open. I'm swallowed in emotion and fight back the tears. I don't want to get too happy just yet, and then I hear Gloria's voice: *'Get a grip of yourself, man! You're a snivelling mess lately. You never used to be like this. "Keep it real," as the kids say. If you're going to do this, then do it with conviction…'*

No, Gloria wouldn't say that; she'd simply disown me if she knew what I was up to. Maybe she does?

With trepidation, I slip inside the main gates. I stick to a route I know like the back of my hand, but The Berry probably not. It doesn't have cameras, unlike the main thoroughfare. I weave in and out of cages and enclosures, listening to the hisses, growls, grunts, and snores in the darkness. It's amazing how quiet the zoo is at night. Not even the howler monkey bothers to howl.

A minute later, I'm at Sinbad's enclosure. I insert the other key into the elephant house lock and, surprise, surprise, it opens the gate as if it had opened it a thousand times before. I can't believe how smooth this is running. In the elephant house, I hear the deep sighs of the elephants as they sleep. There's nothing more pleasing to the ear. But *my* elephant, Sinbad, is standing in the corner chewing hay.

I can see his great, hulking mass silhouetted in the darkness. I'm so familiar with these elephants that I can tell them apart just by how they snore.

'Sinbad, it's me…' I produce a Snickers from my anorak pocket and crinkle the wrapper.

The enormous black shadow wades over to me and I can't contain my happiness as I feel Sinbad's trunk snuffling at my face. He hugs me like an old friend would and I laugh and giggle like a kid. 'Breaking in here has been worth it, old boy.'

Suddenly, my own words make me very aware that I am breaking and entering. A bad feeling washes over me. I've never broken the law in my life. No, I tell a lie: I once ran a red light. I begin to panic. I need to get out of here, but how can I leave my elephant now?

With the light from my phone screen, I walk to the back of Sinbad and inspect the damage. A whimper escapes me when I see that Sinbad's rump has been butchered. It wasn't a simple case of being stabbed by a pitch-fork. No, it looked as if the pitch-fork had been driven into Sinbad's flesh and twisted when it hit bone. This injury was no accident; it was deliberate. And my poor elephant never complains as he licks the last of the Snickers toffee from around his teeth.

Reader, there was a moment, just back there, when I was beginning to regret ever coming here, but now I know I have to save my elephant; I won't get a chance because the next time, one of us will be dead. I will not forsake my friend.

As you can gather, Reader, by now, I've completely side-lined a simple midnight visit to my old friend. Tonight there's gonna be a jail-break, as the *Thin Lizzy* song goes. Drastic times call for drastic measures and I've nothing to lose anymore. Maybe I've known from the moment I found the keys Smiler left for me.

It's now or never…

71

I produce another bar of chocolate from my bottomless anorak pocket, tear it open, and wave it in front of Sinbad in the darkness. 'Come, Sinbad.'

He walks forward and reaches out his trunk, but I walk towards the main doors. He follows on behind me…

'Sshh!' I whisper, but how can you tell an elephant to be quiet? I can't help but giggle to myself – a concoction of everything bubbling to the surface now: adrenaline, relief, happiness, and a pinch or two of a secret ingredient which I don't know myself.

If only Gloria could see me now. No, maybe she shouldn't. Her ghost might be standing at the main gates, waiting to turn me back before I get in any deeper than I already am.

I lead Sinbad outside. We cross the enclosure and make our way down through the zoo, Sinbad stretching for the Snickers (the old dangling carrot trick) while I pray The Berry doesn't finish his midnight breakfast ahead of schedule. We come the same way I had come to avoid the cameras. I quicken pace, waving the Snickers like a madman while we march along at a good clip. I watch our shadows cast on the ground by the moonlight; beautiful night for an elephant-kidnapping, Reader. Right now, I have no idea what I'm going to do once we exit the main gates (if we get that far), but I just cannot go back…

Now something happens which hadn't surfaced in the vague plan in my head.

The animals start to howl, whoop, bray, squawk and scream into the night…They want to come with us. The macaws start up with a terrible racket. Then the donkeys kick in, *hee-hawing*. All hell breaks loose when the howler monkeys sound their alarm. The big cats growl in the distance and the wolves bay at the moon. It's like being on all seven continents at once. The laughing hyenas are the last to join the chorus, screaming laughter at me, but I'm not laughing: I've got sweat running down the crack of my ass. Sorry to project that image on you at this late hour, Reader.

Believe me, I would love to bring them all. Just because I worked in a Victorian zoo all my life doesn't mean I don't understand their plight...

Or maybe the animals have spotted Sinbad making a break for it and they're trying to alert The Berry... bastards.

With my heart in my mouth (a cliché, but that's how it feels), I break into a run, frantically waving the Snickers behind me. I drop it from my clumsy hands, scramble around the ground, and retrieve it before Sinbad tramples me...

Even in half-darkness, I see Sinbad limping behind me and I feel his pain with every stride. 'C'mon my friend.' I beckon him on.

I've got the main entrance in my sights now. 'Just a few more steps to go!' I call to Sinbad, as if we were over the border once we get outside the main gates. I know there's no way of dodging the cameras here, not with an elephant at least. There's nothing I can do about it, just make sure that we finish this. I'm in trouble anyway, and they'll know straight away who they're looking at in their camera screens tomorrow morning. So might as well make it worth it, Reader.

I reach the gate and make to open it, realizing that I'd locked it behind me after coming in. 'Fucking moron!'

I fumble for my set of keys. I'm shaking and what would normally take a second is taking forever. Other exotic animals join in the cacophony behind me, adding to the pressure. Do they want me to triumph or fail? I think of prisoners and come to the conclusion (wishful thinking) that the animals want us to break our way to freedom because that gives them hope...

I find the key, drop it, then drop it again, pick it up, stick it in the lock, and twist. The gate swings wide and we stride nto the street outside; man and elephant. What a strange experience seeing my elephant following me across the street… Thankfully, this area is quiet at night. I glimpse across the street at the Chinese restaurant. If anybody should appear at that lit door now, it would be sweet 'n sour elephant for the midnight special. This is crazy, Reader. This is nuts! I've got the balls of a brass monkey!

I lead Sinbad through the main gates of Phoenix Park – his old stomping ground. I pass a couple of homeless people drinking something so strong that the hallucination of an elephant doesn't distract them, but their dogs do sniff at the air.

I lead Sinbad across an open plain, to a copse of oak trees.

Once out of view, I relax – no, I don't relax – I just buy time before continuing on. My plan hadn't played out this far in my head. In a way, my plan ends here.

'Shit, I've left the gate open!' I tell Sinbad. 'Technically, it doesn't matter now, but closing the gate will buy us time; The Berry will never know that an elephant has just been stolen.' I command Sinbad. 'Stay!' and give him the chocolate. The last thing in the world I want now is to cross to the zoo, but I do it, lithely on foot, like a cat burglar. No, more of a drunken cat wearing studded boots. I'm *loud*, Reader. I just can't seem to do things quietly, no matter how lightly I go.

I approach the gates and get my keys ready; this time I don't fumble. I'm more in control now. I pull the gate shut and lock it. Just as I take the key out of the lock, The Berry appears. He's on the phone. I'm standing there in front of him and for some ungodly reason, he doesn't see me. I freeze, just like a kid playing musical-chairs. I try to blend into the ornate steelwork of the gate as a chameleon would, but without the colour change because I'm ghostly pale right now.

The Berry is laughing on the phone and passes by without recognizing me.

I cross back over to Phoenix Park, just short of an underwear change.

Sinbad hasn't moved from where I left him. We stall in the swaying trees. The wind has really gotten up and I'm beginning to wonder if all of this is just an omen of things to come. We stand in the dancing shadows and I don't know *what* the fuck I'm going to do. So, I spark up a cigarette and take this opportunity to give Sinbad the hug I've been wanting to give him since I was forced to retire. I hold onto his tapering trunk as if I was dangling over a cliff, and in a way, Reader, I think I am: falling into the dark oblivion of memory-loss.

'Sinbad, I'm not sure if Mick Munroe kidnapped you or Mick 'Alzheimers'' Munroe…'

Sinbad is busy negotiating toffee remainders on his molars…

'But as far as I know, Alzheimer's doesn't change your personality – it makes you forget your personality. So, on that basis, maybe the Alzheimer's is to blame? But I don't think so: this is me.' I look into the eyes of my elephant. 'I think my heart is to blame.' Off in the distance, I can see the lights of the zoo. 'I'm beginning to think that closing the gate behind us was a *very* good idea. It's bought us time. So, now what do we do, Sinbad? Hmm?'

Here I am, standing in the middle of a park in Dublin, trying to hide an elephant. I laugh nervously at the thoughts of that, and I *think* I see a smirk on Sinbad's toffee-drooping lip.

Another fifteen minutes passes by in a flash. I'm in some kind of delirious, adrenaline-fuelled time-warp, not believing what I have done tonight, but it's time to make a decision. I look up at my old friend and stare him in the eyes as the oak trees sway and whoosh around us. Thunder rolls off in the distance.

'Should we stay or should we go now?' Tonight is beginning to turn into the soundtrack of my sixty odd years on this planet. Tonight is, I feel, the culmination of my life, Reader. Okay, enough reflection; I need to think about our immediate future.

'If we go back now,' I tell Sinbad, 'then my punishment might be less severe, but it would all have been for nothing. And…'

Sinbad suddenly begins to saunter off in the opposite direction to the zoo and I take this as the *'…go'* part of The Clash's masterpiece.

'I guess you've just made up my mind for me.'

With my heart in danger of imploding, I make the decision to follow my elephant – follow him to the ends of the Earth if that's what it takes. I'm all in, Reader. But to get to the ends of the Earth, we first need to get out of Phoenix Park.

Smiler's Rescue Deal

I have a serious dilemma, Reader. There's no way that I can get away with hiding an elephant in Dublin City. No, I'm serious – the city is small, but six hundred thousand people are a lot of eyes. I'd do the math, but it was never my strong point.

I think and think, spark up another ciggie, and come to the same conclusion: 'Sinbad, we have no choice but to ring Smiler.'

Sinbad stands in the shadows, idly searching overhead branches with his trunk. It's all new to him. He's like a kid in a sweet-shop.

'Smiler's got some other very interesting keys and not just the keys he left for me tonight to get to you.' I speak to Sinbad, but it also helps me think. 'Smiler happens to be the main zoo-driver. He drives the big juggernaut the zoo uses to transport large animals when needs be. He's got access to that special trailer used for the African savannah animals, and I include your big-eared relative, the African elephant.'

With trembling hands, I call Smiler. I'm getting this déjà vu of when I was possibly eighteen years old, ringing my parents at three in the morning to come and get me in the police station because I had been picked up drunk in charge of a bicycle. The embarrassment, Reader.

I wonder if I am doing the right thing as I listen to the dial tone of Smiler's phone. It takes him a while to answer, of course it does: it's the middle of the night. There's some rustling before I hear Smiler's voice reaffirming my thoughts, but a tad more vehemently:

'This better be good. It's the middle of the fucking night, Mick. What's up?'

'I'm in a bit of a pickle. That's putting it mildly.'

'Can it wait till tomorrow?'

I look up at Sinbad. 'Probably not.'

'Oh Jesus,' Smiler sighs, 'what have you done now? You've murdered him?'

'Who?'

'Bean…'

'Christ, no. It's a lot worse than that – nobody would miss him.'

'What does that mean?'

'It's a long story. Can you meet me?'

I hear Smiler sighing down the line at me.

'Sorry, but I wouldn't ask if I didn't have to. You're my last option.'

'Ok,' Smiler drones, 'I'll be down in twenty minutes.'

'No, I'm not at home.'

'Oh, here we go. So, where are you?'

'The zoo…*near* the zoo.'

I hear Smiler lip his favourite turn-of-phrase: '*Sweet Jesus…*' Then, 'Mick, is there something you're not telling me?'

Smiler sure is putting up a good show; he left the keys for me, after all. He knows and he's carrying on for the benefit of this telephone call that will be later analysed for evidence.

I'm stuck for words. 'Yeah, there is…'

'Gimme a minute.'

Smiler doesn't wait for pleasantries and hangs up immediately.

I call him back. 'How're you going to get from your place to the zoo in a minute?'

'I'm *at* the zoo – sleeping with the monkeys.'

A wild burst of laughter escapes me. 'Again?'

'It's no laughing matter, Mick. I should've just gone home when I left The Sod, but I ran into a few old mates and we got a little drunk. I didn't even bother going home to Kelly – straight to the monkeys.'

He hangs up for the second time.

We wait. I keep an eye for Smiler appearing at the zoo-gates while Sinbad discovers new aromas.

'That's the smell of freedom, old boy.' It lifts my heart seeing him free like this, experiencing something he has never experienced. Yes, he was free a few nights ago, but he didn't have time to relax and savour what it is to be free. I'm happy he broke loose because we might not be here now. And, in a way, I'm happy that I've broken free. Take this line-of-thinking a little further and I can thank the Alzheimer's for tonight…

From my vantage point in Phoenix Park, I see Smiler appear at the gates with the same clothes he had when we went for a few drinks at The Sod earlier – he'd hardly have his pyjamas on with the monkeys, I suppose.

I whistle to Smiler, but he can't hear me over the wind, so I whistle him with my thumb and forefinger…

Smiler looks over his shoulder into the darkness of the oak copse in Phoenix Park, but turns away again. He doesn't know it's me; he's expecting to meet me on the street.

I get back on the phone and ring him. I see him pick up.

'That's me whistling.'

'Why are you hiding in the trees? In Phoenix Park?'

'Just follow the light of my phone. Follow the light…'

Smiler repeats this, 'Follow the light…' curses under his breath, and hangs up.

I wave my phone screen. Across the way, Smiler locks on and comes my way.

He enters the copse. 'What are you doing here?' He looks at me…then Smiler's eyes widen in the darkness as he sees Sinbad's outline a few meters beyond me. 'Please tell me that's a big cow or something…' He stares at me with the whites of his eyes bulging from their sockets.

'I don't think you'd believe me if I told you that it's a big cow.'

'No.' Smiler walks up to me in a daze. 'What have you done, Mick? *What* have you done?!'

'Tonight there's gonna be a jail-break, Smiler.'

Smiler blesses himself. Things *must* be bad. 'Sweet Mary, mother of Jesus…'

'I refuse to let my elephant be abused by that fucking moron. We've spent too much time together. I just can't be at home anymore, Smiler. I need to save him…and he's saved me tonight. I'm happy.'

'Oh, that makes it all dandy. Great, you're happy.'

'Now don't get all sarcastic with me.'

'I can think of other ways to be happy, but it doesn't involve kidnapping an elephant.'

'I can't.'

Smiler sighs and almost looks relieved. 'I thought…' he pauses.

'What?'

'I thought you were lost. Y'know, couldn't remember your way home…couldn't remember how you've gotten here…That would've scared me shitless – it's a relief finding an elephant.' He laughs nervously. 'Never thought I'd say that.'

We both smile.

'My mind is sharper than it ever was. Anyway, don't play innocent with me.'

'What do you mean?'

'You left those keys so I'd find them.'

'What keys?'

'The keys you left on the table at The Sod.'

'*You* have them? Oh, thank Christ for that! I thought one of the chimpanzees had gotten hold of them. That would be chaos. They'd try every door at the zoo till they found the right lock and make their escape.'

I'm confused. 'You didn't plant them?'

'No. Why would I? Long has given me the keys cos,' Smiler becomes a little awkward, 'I've been given a promotion. I'm in the office now.'

I'm a little gutted that I was never promoted, but I congratulate Smiler all the same.

Smiler's face turns to horror. 'And there goes my fucking promotion, Mick!'

'We both know that your promotion is going to last a few weeks tops because you love your monkeys and you hate paperwork – monkeys and paperwork are not compatible. Give a chimp a filing-cabinet and see what happens.'

'True, but when they find out that I was an accomplice to this, I'll lose my job. What about my itineraries that I'm waiting to go on? What about my almost ex-wife? I have a list this long,' measuring a meter of air in front of his face. 'That means *money*, Mick.'

'Smiler, my intention is to get nobody in trouble – just myself. I took those keys out of your pocket when you went to the counter for a round of drinks.'

'Huh? Why did you –'

'It's not *true*, Smiler. You left them on the seat and I thought that you'd left them there for me, but that was a lack of foresight on my behalf.'

'That's called severe *short-sightedness* where I come from, Mick!'

'Maybe somebody else caused those keys to fall from your pocket and me to find them?' I don't want to say my Glow's spirit, but I can't help thinking it.

'Now you're giving me the creeps.'

Smiler's taken the wind out of my sails. I was sure he'd left those keys there for me to kidnap my elephant. Isn't it funny how your mind can convince you of the opposite? Now, I'm not so sure about asking Smiler for his help. 'So why all that info about The Berry going for midnight breakfast and all that?'

81

Smiler pauses. 'I thought you might've gone up there after the few pints when I left you. Just to check in with him and see how everything is. Get on his good side and ask for a sneak-peek of your elephant.'

I completely read it wrong.

'Mick, why did you call me out here?'

'I'm not coming back, Smiler – we're not coming back.'

Smiler blinks and shakes my words around in his head to see if he can jumble them up and understand them a different way. 'I don't get it.'

'I came here thinking that I would just visit my elephant and say one last goodbye because it hurts too much to see him like he was. But I couldn't turn my back on him. I have nothing left at home and he has nothing left at the zoo. I need something to remember when the Alzheimer's takes over and I reckon if I can remember this adventure and Gloria, then I'm happy to let the rest fizzle away. I always knew there was one last ride.' I decide to cut to the chase. 'Speaking of rides; I need the truck, Smiler. We need you to get us out of here.'

Smiler's stuck for words. He clasps his hands around the back of his head and stares at the branches overhead.

'Just a few miles out,' I try convincing him. 'Get us out into the countryside and we'll work from there. I have my bank card so I can use ATMs along the way. I'll need to pack a bag. I can buy clothes if I need them.'

'You've lost your mind!'

'Not yet, but getting there.'

'Okay, so that was an unfortunate turn of phrase. I mean, what are you going to do, Mick? Go looking for bargains in *Primark*? You might get away with a Chihuahua in a handbag, but not an elephant. *How* are you going to hide the elephant? Listen to me… I can't believe I'm actually saying this.'

'I'll face that when I come to it.'

'I recommend you start thinking about it.' Smiler keeps shaking his head. 'I don't know, Mick. I just don't know what to say.'

'Say yes…I need the truck.'

'What truck?'

'The zoo truck. The one you're asked to drive every now and again.'

'You're *insane*, Mick. Forget Alzheimer's!'

'I don't have any hope while we're here in Dublin. Just get me out of the park and down-country a few miles and drop us off. We'll stick to the by-roads.'

'Drop us off? Drop us *off?!* Mick, you're travelling with an elephant; that has consequences. What will you do, hitch-hike around the country? I wouldn't let a stranger sit into my car, never mind an elephant.'

'Please, George.'

I don't use his real name often. Does that mean something? I think so…

Smiler's in a real predicament now. He goes off into the undergrowth. I presume it's to think, but he takes a piss instead. 'It just so happens,' he says as he christens some nettles, 'that I've got the keys right here.'

I hear him jingle the keys. Something about the way Smiler is speaking tells me that he had planned this whole thing. Now I don't know what to think. 'I'll never ask you to do anything ever again, promise. Look on it as the most important itinerary of your life.'

'Don't toy with my emotions, Mick.'

I spark up another cigarette off my previous smouldering butt-end. 'Smiler, I need an answer in the next few seconds. I want to be out in the countryside in an hour's time and settle down for the night in some barn.'

'Please! Like I said; I'm already in too far to back out now, so I'm going to go out with a bang.'

'Exactly, Mick, *Bang Bang Chitty Chitty Bang Bang*…I think you've been watching too many Disney films.'

Without warning, but maybe it had been sneaking up on me, I suddenly lose my immediate memory and cannot, for the life of me, remember what I had been doing.

'Mick, what is it?'

'Huh?' Gazing around me, all I see are trees and it's the middle of the night. 'Where am I? What's happening?' I see a man standing in front of me and I'm not sure what I'm doing here with him. My mind is all fuzzy. I try to dig deep into my memory vault, but memory *fault* is all I find.

'Mick. It's okay. Just relax a minute.'

He knows me…

'I'm Smiler – George – and we worked with each other at the zoo for many years. You called me out here tonight to give you a hand.'

'With what?'

George, AKA Smiler, pauses before raising his eyebrows at something behind me.

I turn to see…an elephant.

This individual is clearly out of his depth and would prefer to be somewhere – *anywhere* – else. 'Mick,' he calls me, 'you have Alzheimer's. Do you have medication?'

'I don't know.'

'Search your pockets.'

I do so and produce several Snickers.

'No,' answers the man, 'that's *his* medication. Don't you have pills or something?'

I dig deeper and produce a familiar dark brown, capped tube of pills.

He takes the bottle from me and squints to read it, but curses that he doesn't have his magnifying glass. He holds the medication up to his right eye and reads: 'To be taken three times a day with meals, it says here. Are you doing that, Mick? These pills are called gal…galtan…galantamine or something like that.'

I'm all confused. 'I think so. I, I don't know.' I wander over to the elephant in a dizzy haze. The elephant caresses me with its trunk. The feeling is exquisite and gives me the shivers. The shivers are so intense that my arms and neck prick in goose-bumps. Then I begin to realize where I am. The whole scenario becomes familiar and I remember why I'm here. 'Sinbad?'

'That's right.' Smiler visibly wilts in front of me. 'Jesus, thought I'd lost you there, man. Don't *do* that to me! Y'know I hate medical stuff and hospitals. Please, take your *fucking* meds. I don't do mouth-to-mouth…'

'Okay…'

'Sorry. I just can't handle that shit.'

'So, where was I?'

'It's crazy to say it, but I think Sinbad tapped into your circuit-board and flicked some switches or something like that.'

'What?'

'Dunno, Mick, I'm not medically-minded. Sinbad had an affect over you. You were lost till he started,' Smiler wiggles his fingers, 'touching you with his trunk. It was all mystic 'n shit.'

My memory comes back in little pixels, but I still don't have the full picture; I still can't recall why we are here. 'What were we doing?'

Smiler falters. 'We were about to hide an elephant…'

I remember! 'So, you're in!?' I ask with undeniable hope.

Smiler sighs deeply. 'I'll be honest with you. I was this close,' cue little space between thumb and forefinger, 'to telling you that we were about to take this escaped elephant back to the zoo, but I've got too much respect for you. Maybe I'm an old, sentimental fool.'

'Yes, you are.'

'Maybe a true friend would stop you. Maybe a true friend would let you go…dunno.'

We share a smile, though my lapse of memory has left me shook and scared. I try to give the impression that it's

85

no big deal. If I make too much of it, Smiler won't agree. I'm already counting my lucky stars that he has agreed.

Smiler takes a deep breath. 'Okay, I'll do this but on one condition.'

'And that is? No weird shit…'

'You stole the keys of the truck as well.'

I happily agree to Smiler's terms. 'I'm in over my head already anyway. Do you want me to admit to murder too? Who do you want me to kill?'

Smiler answers readily, 'I can think of a few on my hit-list.'

'Me too.'

'Let's just try and hide the elephant for now.'

Without further ado, Smiler crosses Phoenix Park. 'Don't go anywhere.'

Hardly able to breath with excitement, I watch Smiler open the truck and climb up into the cab. A second later, the truck rumbles into life and the headlights come my way. Smiler flashes them, which I take as my cue to get ready…

'Come, Sinbad…'

I emerge out of the shadows with Sinbad at my heels on the scent of another Snickers. I'm glad I bought that bumper-pack. I'll have to stock up ASAP somewhere along the road – listen to me, oh, mercy!

Smiler flashes his lights again. I'm beginning to wonder what's with all the headlight drama when I see The Berry appear next to the truck…

I freeze…But Sinbad's all trunk, looking for the chocolate…

'Stop! Stop Sinbad!' *Stop* was one of the first commands I taught Sinbad, funnily enough.

Over the wind, I barely make out The Berry asking Smiler what he's up to so late at night. Smiler explains that he's getting things ready for the morning's drive South to Fota Island with a giraffe.

'At three in the morning?' The Berry asks.

Meanwhile, Sinbad is performing a strip-search on me to find the Snickers…

Smiler tells The Berry that he's suffering from insomnia (monkeys keeping him awake) and that if he got everything ready now, then that would give him an extra hour in bed in the morning. 'Might as well be doing something as staring up at the ceiling.'

The Berry stalls. 'Wait, you've sneaked into the monkeys tonight, haven't you? Just cos you have wife-trouble doesn't mean to say that I have to lose my job. You know I can't allow…'

'I'll treat you to a fortnight of Chinese if you just overlook that delicate detail. It won't happen again, promise.'

The Berry laughs and accepts two weeks-worth of sweet 'n sour chicken which is a little worrying.

The Berry goes back inside and Smiler sits there in the truck for a moment, probably trying to calm his heart down.

I wait, fixed to the spot, until Smiler flashes his lights again. I continue across the grass and pull up in the shadows of a giant horse chestnut. Smiler reverses the truck as close as possible to the gates of Phoenix Park and lets down the ramp. I coax my elephant up the ramp by giving him a sniff of chocolate – I think Sinbad would walk over the edge of a cliff if he saw a Snickers floating in mid-air, which drives home the succinct point that, ultimately, I'm in this alone. It's not as if Sinbad begged me to get him out; he's just coming along for this last ride.

'Now you've got me in a whole pile of shit!' Smiler's not impressed. 'You see, now I'm transporting a stolen elephant instead of an invisible giraffe… Sweet Jesus, Mary Mother of God…' Smiler slams up the ramp behind us. I giggle to myself in the confines of the truck while Sinbad tucks into some hay from the hay nets. I make sure

Sinbad is comfortable, then exit through the side-door and join Smiler in the cab.

'Won't The Berry hear us driving off?'

Smiler thinks about this. 'True.' He climbs down and lithely tip-toes back to the zoo gates. I watch him in the side-mirror come back to the truck.

'He's too busy watching a film on his laptop.'

'You do realize you've just put The Berry to death by offering free Chinese grub for two weeks?'

'Nah, he'll be fine. My problem is Kelly. She'll go *crazy* if she finds out about this.'

'Your wife *will* go crazy if you tell her. Simple equation, Smiler.'

We pull out of the car-park with haste. Once clear of the zoo confines, Smiler informs me that he's got a simple itinerary worked out.

'Can we add my place to your itinerary?'

'You sure that's a good idea?'

'I need to pack a few things.'

'Jeeesus, Mick. Are we doing the right thing? No, let me rephrase that: are you doing the right thing cos I know *I'm* doing the wrong thing.'

We drive on through the quiet streets and pull up as close to my place as we can without getting into difficulties with the truck. I run in home and pack a few essentials into a backpack I had left out for my trip to Denmark and Scotland; essentials mainly comprising of a flashlight and all the guilt-*Snickers* I had bought after being fired. I also pack the duty-free 200-pack of cigarettes Smiler had brought me from one of his undiscovered European destinations. Maybe I can kick the habit on this little adventure or else I'll come back smoking double. Either is a possibility at this stage. And as a last minute decision, I bring the Canon digital camera Gloria bought me on my 58th birthday – the last one we would share together. I haven't felt this excited since I was a kid. Reader, I actually give a quick tidy up in the living-room before I leave; fix the cushions in their right place and straighten up the place a little. Just to have the place nice when the police break in.

Then, I decide to bring a new journal. I fling it into the backpack. This is a new chapter of my life – a new *book*, rather. A symbolic change from a daily hum-drum diary to this story/diary/account/tour guide/*How to Hide Your Elephant for Dummies.*

I look back over my shoulder at my living-room, see my miniatures, my clocks, the Post-Its, and my old diary on the living-room table. I switch out the light without regrets.

I climb into the cab.

Smiler is frowning behind the wheel. 'Y'know, I was thinking while you were gone.'

'Is that a good or bad sign?'

'It's a sign that I could be done for drunk-driving. I was in the pub only an hour ago.'

'You seem to be in control.'

'Ah, lots of years of experience.'

'Yeah. I want to head southwest.'

'What's down there?'

'An island…The Blasket Islands. Glow and myself visited the place once and it was pure magic. Some of the country's finest writers were born on that little island…'

'Sweet Jeeeesus, Mick. Take Sinbad across on the ferry, will you?'

'I'll face that problem when I come to it.'

We take the southbound motorway out of the capital. We drive in silence. The city lights become less and less until we are in the darkness of the open countryside.

An hour and a half later, Smiler turns off the motorway and drives down a narrow country road somewhere in County Tipperary and, apparently, the end of our itinerary. 'End of the line, kid.'

I reach out my hand and shake Smiler's hand. 'You're a good friend.'

'You're on your own, Mick. I won't be coming back for you. There's too much at stake…job…wife. I can't even believe I'm doing this.'

I get out and we let down the back ramp on the side of a narrow country lane. I coax Sinbad out of the truck and we say goodbye to Smiler.

When we shake hands, I tell my friend that we'll probably see each other in a few days from now, but not specifying where or under what circumstances. It just sounds reassuring and *normal*.

'Sinbad, come…' We walk away.

Smiler stops me. 'Where you going?'

'Southwest…' I answer vaguely. 'I told you.'

Smiler mutters, 'Sweet Jesus,' to himself, then points in the opposite direction. 'Southwest is that way.'

I wave a thank-you and head off in the opposite direction.

Smiler calls me before my elephant and I melt into the night. 'I did leave those keys. You didn't imagine anything. I felt guilty, that's why I helped you tonight. Though I thought you'd only make a visit to Sinbad when I left those keys, not kidnap him.'

I knew it! 'Why guilty?'

Smiler pauses. 'It was me who told Long about your string of minor little fuck ups – your forget-me-nots.'

I can't believe what I'm hearing. 'Why would you do that?'

'Because I was concerned, Mick. You've always been so meticulous at work, never miss a trick. Suddenly, you're leaving cages open and leaving equipment lying around where you shouldn't. I did it cos I was worried. There was no badness behind it.'

'You could've told me.'

'I did. I mentioned it several times in passing, not wanting to make a big deal out of it, but you didn't listen or forgot. I knew there was something major up. We've both known Long many years and I told him as a friend to keep an eye on you. My plan sort of back-fired. I didn't think it would get to HR. But I think I'm back in your good books now?'

'You are.' I nod and wave him goodbye. I understand; I would've done the same for Smiler.

'I'll see you on the news,' jokes Smiler and gets back in the zoo truck.

It's just my elephant and me now.

Origami Elephant

Smiler pulls away, and I watch the red rear-lights recede into the night and disappear around a bend. I didn't think he would've left so abruptly, but there's nothing left to say.

I switch on my flashlight, but switch it off again, mainly because the sky is clear and the full moon is bathing the countryside in eerie celestial silver.

By the light of the moon, I search my backpack for a Snickers and break it in half. It won't be as easy to run down to the corner-shop as it was at home, so Sinbad will be on rations from here on in. I give him the chocolate and command him to follow on. 'Come, Sinbad…'

It takes a few minutes for my nerves to settle and I begin to enjoy my walk in the dead-hour. Step by step, I become more ecstatic, Reader, as Sinbad and I ease into a steady walking pace towards who-knows-where. There's something apocalyptic about tonight: are we running from or to something?

It's a bright night and I've always had good eyesight. I have never seen such profound darkness because there's always light in the city, but I'm amazed at how much I can see without the aid of daylight. It's not as windy as it was back in Dublin, but it's bitterly cold and save for a few wispy clouds passing across the face of the moon, it's a clear night full of stars – hopefully, my lucky stars. My old man and I spent hours star-gazing, but the light of the city always killed starlight. If my old man was here now he'd marvel at this clear, crisp night. I quickly make out The Plough constellation and the direction I'm moving along it. I take a mental photo. I may need it later should I get lost.

Reader, you might be thinking right about now that I've completely lost the plot, but you must understand that I don't give two flying monkeys if I'm caught; every step forward is a triumph as far as I'm concerned and we're going to enjoy our freedom while we can. In a way, I've already accomplished what I set out to do tonight and that was to spend some bonding time with Sinbad, just the two of us. You see, we'll both end up behind bars anyway.

Down in a valley, I spot what looks to be a farm, some outhouses, and a main house with a light on. I think I see a barn a little way off from the farm and decide to take refuge there for what's left of the night. Hopefully we can hold up there tomorrow without being seen. Listen to me, I'm talking like an on-the-run fugitive…I suppose I am: a fugitive of the times.

'C'mon, Sinbad…' I whisper, realizing that I'm down in a valley, out in the middle of nowhere and I could shout to the heavens if I wanted to.

So I do!

I whoop and holler to my heart's content. My screams of joy echo around the valley of happiness, even Sinbad gets in on the act and trumpets with his trunk held high. Tears of joy come. What a sentimental old fool I am.

Quickly realizing that could be a mistake, I shush him to be quiet. It's one thing to have a lunatic screaming at three in the morning in the countryside, but quite something else to have an Indian elephant screaming in the Irish countryside at three in the morning.

We make it to the barn. I fumble with the slide-door before pulling it across on its hinges. I flinch as the door squeals on its rusty wheels. The last thing I need now is a sleepy family coming out to their barn in the middle of the night to find a crazed, old lunatic and an elephant. My plan, should that happen, is try convince them that they're having a collective dream/nightmare.

It's almost pitch dark and I can't see anything inside the barn. Behind me, Sinbad begins to wander off. 'Get back here!' I struggle to keep my voice to a whisper… I scramble around the dark, my fingers searching for anything that resembles a light switch. I find a switch, far too high to be taken seriously, and flick it downwards. The hay-barn is thrown into magnificent warm light, far too bright for my liking. My heart lifts when I see a barn half-full of hay. Over in the other corner, sectioned off by some enormous expanses of plastic sheets, are some lambs. They begin to bleat and I ask them kindly to be quiet. The hay-barn is compartmentalised with great sheets of heavy black plastic that form temporary rooms, running off a system of wires attached to the low eaves of the barn. Why? No idea. There is also an old sink. I check the tap and it works. I quickly locate a bucket and fill it for Sinbad.

Sinbad doesn't need an official invitation as he wades into the hay-barn, looking enormous under the roof. It's the perfect place to stay the night. He siphons off the bucket of water in seconds and looks for another bucket, and then another. Having had his fill of water, he sidles up next to the hay and begins to pluck at it. I laugh nervously to myself, not quite believing what is happening, and pull the door shut to the same horrible squeal.

I switch out the light and lie down on some hay, high enough on the hay stack not to get trampled by Sinbad. I listen to the sounds of the barn: my elephant chewing on hay while the lambs bleat softly. This moment – *this* moment – has made everything worth it. If I could just live here forever.

Famous last words…

Voices wake me. For a moment, I'm sure that they are only in my dreams and am happy enough to wallow in my slumber. But as I surface from a deep sleep, I quickly realize that the voices are right outside the barn door – children's voices.

Oh, mercy!

They're playing outside in the yard. I check my watch and curse to the high Heavens, seeing that I overslept. I *never* oversleep. I've had the best night's sleep since I can remember. It's almost nine in the morning! Sinbad is lying down, looking content and relaxed. But have I overslept?

Not really because I'm not late for anything; my plan is to stay here till afternoon when dusk falls. But in my absurd planning, somebody visiting the barn isn't an option. My plan has got a crazy dreamlike logic to it. If I'm lucky enough, it might happen, but I'm thinking that I'll be back on the truck to the zoo within the hour.

The kids begin to fiddle around the handle of the door.

I jump to my feet too fast and grow dizzy. I command Sinbad to get up as I've done a thousand times before at the zoo. He does so with an old-man grunt and groan. I panic and do a great Bean impression by trying to push my elephant beyond one of those large curtain things that section off the barn. I'm wasting my time: Sinbad's rules or no rules. I dig in my pockets, cursing Sinbad at the same time for his stubbornness, and coax him with an empty wrapper (it's all I can find in the heat of the moment). It works! I lure him behind one of the sheets, just in time as the door rolls back and three kids march into the barn, a boy and two girls.

I watch them cross in front of me, completely oblivious to the strangers in their barn. They've got a bottle of milk and begin to feed the lambs, giggling and arguing at every opportunity as kids do. I stay as quiet as possible, but Sinbad decides that it's a good moment to start siphoning the water dregs from one of the three buckets I had left the night before. A long, agonizing, sucking fills the barn.

The kids stop and look around…

I freeze as six little eyes fix on the dusty, old plastic that keeps me hidden from the world. For all they know, there's a giant behind here, sitting on a pile of hay bales, finishing the last of his strawberry bucket milk-shake through a straw the size of a PVC gutter pipe.

They approach the sheet and stall. I hear them whispering, before the boy, maybe eight or nine years old, pulls open the curtain. The two girls, a little younger, stand there and look at me. I'm lost for words as they are. It's almost comical. What do I say? *Don't worry, you're all only imagining that there's an elephant in your barn…*

'Sshh!' I signal. 'It's a secret, okay.'

"Secret" grabs their interest. At least, that's what I think until the youngest girl's bottom lip drops and I know there's a blood-curdling scream coming at me, but her sister (I presume it's her sister because they are almost identical) slaps her mouth around the 'O' shape that's about to siren…

'You're on private property,' the boy informs me with a stern expression.

'Oh, is it?' I'm wondering whether he'll be a policeman or a lawyer when he comes of age because, right now, he's just a kid.

'I'm going to tell our dad there's a strange man in our barn.'

'No, no, you've got it all wrong. I'm not strange…I've been called a lot of things, but *strange* isn't one of them. But I agree that the situation may be a little, let's say, *odd*.' *Smart-ass…*

'Okay, *odd*, then…' The boy is just about to turn away with his sisters in tow when a trunk appears from behind the plastic curtain next to me. The trunk reaches out to them.

Cue the two girls scream that brings the barn down while I beg them to be quiet in agonizing facial gestures. My words go unheard while I pull out a fistful of hair follicles in the process. I pull back the polythene curtain with all the finesse of a show-man and the kids stare up, slack-jawed, at the elephant standing in their barn. The screams are replaced by whimpers, then gulps.

The wide-eyed boy asks, 'Is that real?'

No, it's a stuffed elephant, I want to tell the smart-ass. 'Yep, it's real. This is Si-ammy…' I almost blurt his name out, 'Sammy...Sammy Davis Junior.' I just couldn't leave it at Sammy – I'm nervous, Reader, give me a break. Then again, giving my elephant a false name while on the run is a little pointless as there aren't many on-the-run elephants in the Irish countryside that he can be mistaken for – this isn't New Delhi. A loose elephant doesn't need a name, in other words. 'We are on the run from a bad man who...' should I be even telling them this much? '...wants to hurt Si-ammy. If you tell anybody that we are here, they will just take my elephant back where he came from,' I purposefully omit any details, but again, kind of pointless, 'and the bad man will hurt Sammy again. Please, let's keep the elephant a secret. Is that okay? Um, he likes to eat Snickers...'

The boy studies me before pulling his sisters off to a side to discuss the situation in private. They huddle in a tiny group, occasionally looking over at me over their shoulders and up at the elephant.

With serious little faces, they come back with their decision. I'd laugh if I wasn't so nervous...

The oldest girl says to me in earnest, 'We want to help Sammy. We will keep him a secret.'

'Thank you! You –'

The boy intervenes, 'But we have to tell our parents about you. You're strange...weird, whatever.'

'Huh? *What?!* No, no that's a bad idea, cos, see, without me Si-ammy will go back and the bad man will hurt him. I'm a stranger, yes, but not all strangers are *strange*. See what I'm getting at?'

The kids remain tight-lipped and pensive before the boy walks off, followed by his younger sisters and another barn summit gets underway, hushed opinions going back and forth, before the eldest girl comes up to me. 'Okay.' She holds out her hand and I shake it.

I wipe the sweat from my brow and thank the kids.

The boy asks, 'How long will you be here for?' as if he's

thinking of hiring out the barn to me.

I'm very quick to tell him that Sammy Davis Junior and I will be off his *private property* after sun-down which is between four and five in the evening.

The kid nods with a blank expression. I'm not sure what he's thinking. Then he surprises me by asking me if I want anything to eat. I hadn't realized how hungry I was. I decide to call his bluff. 'I shouldn't take food from strangers…'

He's just about to give me back what I'd just given him about being a stranger before he realizes that I am joking. He reddens up and giggles like the normal, honest kid that he is.

I've broken the ice, Reader.

'I would love something to eat! Anything at all, I don't care…mouldy bread, whatever. Except hay – I'm allergic to hay.'

The girls chuckle at this.

'My name's Gabriel, but you can call me Gabe. These are my sisters Lena and Breda.'

I salute them and tell them my name is…I stall; a fugitive on the run never gives personal details (whatever about the elephant) and I remember, crystal clear, a recent line from my life: 'I'm just a human without resources.'

They don't understand that, going by their mute reactions. Of course they don't. So I cut to the chase. 'How about bringing me something from your fridge?'

The kids swop glances and skitter out of the barn.

Five minutes later they come back with a chunk of cheese, half a loaf of bread, some fresh bacon, and…a pepper. The little one, Lena, is carrying the green pepper. She hands it to me.

I take it and look at it.

'There was nothing left so I brought this.'

I smile and thank her and lay it aside for later if I need to brew some of my own pepper spray – which I'm not ruling out. I spot her DIY necklace. 'That's a pretty necklace.' On a shoe-lace, there is a little witch stirring a cauldron of something.

'It's a wish charm,' she tells me. 'You hold onto this little wish and make a witch.'

Her sister bursts out laughing, blowing the contents of her nose everywhere at the same time…

'I mean, hold onto this…'

I put her out of her misery. 'Don't worry, I know what you mean. Maybe you could make a wish for me?'

'Sure,' says Lena. 'I'll make a wish for you…'

Breda adds, 'Hash tag, *elephant*,' whatever that means.

So, wanting these kids on my side, I hold the little witch and make a wish. I suddenly find myself making a genuine wish. I can't tell you what that wish is, Reader, because it might break the spell if I tell you.

After I make my wish, Lena shatters the moment by adding: 'I'm taking it back to the shop cos my wishes don't come true.'

Gabe kicks in, 'It's a faulty product.'

I *love* kids. 'Now, I know this might sound crazy, but why not wish for an elephant…right here in your barn.'

So Lena does, closes her eyes shut as if her young life depends on it. I lay Sinbad's trunk on her head.

'Now, open your eyes.'

She opens her eyes and they grow wide when she sees Sinbad's wrinkled trunk resting on her head. He then starts to check her out and she giggles as he tickles her.

'Dreams do come true, Lena. We just have to believe they will. And if they don't, then we'll die trying.'

'Or take the faulty product back to the shop and ask for a refund…'

'Yes, Gabe, you're absolutely right.'

Gabe dismisses the whole thing. 'We're going to school now. See you this evening. My father is gone to the cattle market for the day and my mom never comes in here, so you're safe.'

'Thank you.' I know it's only a matter of time before I'm sprung.

I say goodbye to the kids and wish I had grand-children of my own. It must be a real gift so late in life – kind of gives a sense of continuity.

Sorry, I'm rambling.

I spend the rest of the day in the barn. Sinbad is happy, having plenty of room to stretch his legs and water and hay on-hand.

To the children's credit, they don't breathe a word to their parents.

The last time I went to the bathroom as nature intended was when I was a kid. It's a messy business and it was the last thing I had been thinking about last night, sitting in the The Sod, staring longingly at the guilt-keys which Smiler *had* planted. It's a humbling experience to scramble across a farmyard with your trousers down around your ankles, looking for dock-leaves to wipe yourself and dodging the farmer's wife at the same time. It wasn't in my crazy plan, Reader. But then again, those little details never are. Things *never* play out like you plan them. But, I am hiding out on a farm and I have to say that it is *the* adventure of my life-time. If only Gloria could see me now…No, maybe it is better she doesn't see me trying to clean myself on a farmyard. I probably wouldn't be here now if Gloria were still around. You can take that to the bank, Reader. And speaking of banks, I should find an ATM soon…

I take these precious few hours to realize my lifelong dream of climbing aboard Sinbad. My first attempt, back at the zoo, was an embarrassing failure. So, while he's busying himself chomping on hay, I pull myself up onto the shaky tower of bales and lean across with my right hand and find purchase on Sinbad's jutting spine. I launch myself across, now holding on with two hands, forming a human bridge between the elephant and the precarious mountain of hay-bales. My shoes slip and slide on his wrinkled skin, but I manage to find a foothold and lever myself upwards onto his back.

I've done it, Reader! Looks like I was saving the best for last…

Sitting on an elephant's spine isn't the most comfortable, so I pull myself forward and sit in between his ears, behind his head. I laugh like a little kid. Sinbad hardly notices that I'm sitting on his neck. My hands are trembling with nerves. I have so much respect for this friendly giant…

I take my Canon from my anorak pocket and take a few selfies, as they call them. I make several attempts to take the first photo, without success. I need to get a photo of this before Sinbad chucks me off. 'Bear with me, Sinbad…' Eventually, I realize that I'm not pressing the click button correctly. Technology!

Just as I'm about to press the button, the barn door slides open on its rusty rails…

A woman in her forties comes into the barn, humming a tune. She crosses right in front of us, speaking to the lambs. So close, that she could join my selfie. She looks into the pen and watches the lambs for a minute while we stand there, motionless, me at least. Sinbad is oblivious and plucks hay from the hay mountain. The woman presumes its one of their domestic farm animals and doesn't come searching for the Indian elephant.

A phone rings somewhere outside…

The woman doubles back and trots out of the hay-barn, muttering something…

I realize that I've been holding my breath and exhale before I burst.

Sinbad's trunk had been only inches from her behind at one point. If Sinbad's trunk *had* felt her up (this sounds as if the trunk has a mind of its own) and she *had* presumed that it was me, then there *would* be trouble.

Having had enough thrills for one afternoon, I climb/fall/slip from Sinbad onto the hay and sit down to think about my immediate future while wiping more sweat from my brow.

An hour later, I hear kid's voices, before the barn doors slide open. Breda, Lena, and Gabe file into the barn, totally bypassing me and scanning the place for their secret friend, as if checking that they hadn't only dreamt it. They've got their school-bags on their backs. This time, they feel braver and want to get closer to Sinbad. I introduce them. They are amazed with Sinbad. The girls can't stop giggling and the boy just looks up at my elephant with astonishment and I know, by looking at the glint in his eyes, that this is a moment he will never forget and will recall as an older man. I wonder what else he will know about my – our – journey by the time that day comes around? The little one, Lena, suddenly astonishes me by grabbing a hold of Sinbad's trunk and squeezes it in a hug. I haven't seen such love for an elephant since Snuffaleupagus on *Sesame Street*.

'Sammy, can you stay here forever?' she asks Sinbad.

Breda, meanwhile, is recording everything on her phone and playing back our conversation in high-pitch helium voices. She tells me its something called a nap or something similar, called *Talking Tom* – a cat that repeats everything you say in a funny voice. I find it hilarious and speak into it a few times just to hear my helium voice, though I can't believe a child as young as Breda has a phone. We were lucky to have a wireless radio when I was her age. I ask her about it and she tells me that it's her mommy's old phone and that it doesn't work anymore – the calls, at least.

I love these kids…

Breda struts around the barn, speaking to imaginary friends on the other end, occasionally looking at me and miming to me to be quiet because she's busy talking on the phone and all hand gestures. I'm seeing a little pantomime of what probably happens at home. She's hilarious.

'I'd love to stay forever, but Sammy and I need to get going tonight. Somebody will find us if we stay here forever. And anyway, you can't keep stealing food out of your fridge.'

'Awww,' Breda responds and *Talking Tom* repeats her in her pipsqueak voice.

Gabe tells me that they must go for their lunch. 'We'll bring you some cabbage and bacon later.'

I thank him and smile to myself. Nice, nice kids.

The boy hands a Snickers fun-pack to me. 'It's for Sammy Davis Junior. I bought it with my odd-job money. You can never have enough Snickers.'

What a great kid, I think to myself. I check inside the wrapping and count the guts of fifteen mini Snickers. 'These will come in very handy.'

'Can you give him one?'

'Why don't you give it to him yourself?'

Gabe lets his guard down and manages a shy smile; his cool exterior melts. He unwraps the chocolate bar and holds it out to Sinbad, flat on the palm of his hand as if feeding a horse. It's easy to tell that he's a boy who has grown up on a farm. Sinbad quickly sees it, having already heard that opening wrapper, and takes it gently from his hand with precision and curls it back into his gaping mouth.

The kids are awe-struck; the astonished expressions glued to their faces. They look up at Sinbad like I did those first few hours spent with my dad at the zoo all those years ago. What would the old man say now? I dread to think, Reader. I quickly capture the moment with my camera.

There's a call from somewhere outside. 'Lunch, kids…'

The kids turn in unison and file out of the barn. I enjoy their little visits.

Sinbad sits down with a drawn-out, old-man sigh and I

climb up on his back and have a nap…

Maybe Breda had said *app*?

An hour later, the kids return and tell me they've done their homework. They inspect Sinbad, stroke him, and study his tough, furrowed, grey skin before going back outside. Breda shows me her Venus Fly-Trap, putting on a morbid show for all concerned by catching flies in the dusty window panes of the barn and feeding them to the carnivorous plants. Meticulously removing their legs and wings first because the Venus Fly-Trap 'are a little slow for my liking'.

Gabe brings me a lump of salty bacon, a few boiled potatoes, and half a melted cabbage, all doused in the same water it had been boiled in, oh, mercy! I don't know if it's just because I'm on the run or not, but this is the tastiest bacon and cabbage I've eaten since my Glow moved on. I could never get it like Gloria's – she took her secret recipe to the grave.

As I put the final touches on my itinerary, I hear a scream that will stay with me till my dying days, Alzheimer's or not.

Then Gabe bawls, 'Help!' from outside.

I run outside and see that the oldest girl, Breda, has fallen into the slurry pit and is sinking fast. I can hear the other kids yelling for their parents, but nobody's coming…

Without thinking, I run outside in the daylight, forgetting that I'm on-the-run. I sprint up the ramp that runs above and along the slurry pit. I reach down to the girl and she attempts to catch my hand, but the manure is swallowing her and she's out of reach anyway.

A crazy plan B comes to me…

I sprint back to the barn, falling and tumbling all the way.

'Sinbad, c'mon!! Up! Up!'

Sinbad doesn't budge, so I flash the Snickers family-pack in his face. He rises to his feet and I run back across the yard. *'Come, Sinbad!!'*

Sinbad follows at my heels with his trunk raised and ears flapping. He follows me all the way up the ramp. Balancing myself, I grab a hold of his trunk and lean out over the pit. Sinbad's trunk gives a good extra foot to stretch downwards. 'Grab on!' I can see that the girl has hardly any energy left and is struggling to keep her chin above the manure, but she *does* manage to raise her right arm and I grab at the wrist.

'Pull, Sinbad! Pull!'

Sinbad pulls back and Breda comes free of the sucking mire.

She collapses onto the concrete ramp, fatigued and exhausted, covered in foul-smelling dung…but she's alive, Jesus, she's *alive!* I'm shaking all over with fright, not knowing whether to cry or laugh. I just want to get out of here now, *please*. I've overstayed my welcome.

The girl begins to weep uncontrollably while her brother and sister walk around in circles, not knowing what to do.

I tell her that everything is okay, 'though you will need a shower…' I joke, but that's me falling back on my defences. It was so, *so* close, Reader. My hand is shaking as I write these words in my journal.

'Go home, darling, and get cleaned up…'

I ask Gabe and little Lena to help her inside, then I get Breda to her feet and, overjoyed though blubbering, we give each other a hug despite the cow dung. I'd be lying if I told you that I don't cry a little, Reader, cry with relief.

So close to a tragedy… If I hadn't been hiding on this farm, that girl would've died.

The three kids cross the yard, cushioning their sister.

'Hey, Gabe…' I call.

He turns back. The boy is the colour of milk.

'Tell your dad to get a fence put up around this pit…'

Your dad must be a fucking moron… I think to myself.

Gabe nods. I can tell, just by looking at him, that he's just gotten the fright of his life and won't be forgetting today in a hurry.

Suddenly, he runs back to me, gives me a hug and hands me something before running off to his sisters.

I track the kids as they walk up the pathway to the two-story farmhouse (that is much too far away to hear the cries of a kid) before I slump to the ground as the tension and adrenaline of the moment seep away. I'm exhausted and jittery.

My elephant – the hero – stands by my side and I give him the little Snickers.

'I knew those commands I taught you would come in handy,' I tell him.

I pick myself up and we go back inside the barn. I give him a desperate, longing hug. 'You just saved a life, Sinbad. That alone has made this adventure worth it.'

I open my hand to see what Gabe had given me: a paper origami elephant. I understand, Gabe, I really do. If only I could fold up Sinbad and put him in my wallet.

Pot Noodle Hero

We wait another twenty minutes before twilight creeps in. Thankfully, I'm doing this in winter; it's dark before 5pm and that gives us lots of unseen walking-time. I spark up a cigarette and we leave the farm, sticking to the old secondary roads that were once primary. I find that my eyesight very quickly accustoms to the dark. Just like last night, I have little use for my flashlight that I packed, though let's see, pardon the pun, how things go on a cloudy night which is the normal thing in this neck o' the woods. Gabe's cabbage and bacon has been digested long ago and I'm starting to feel the hunger pinch. Sinbad, AKA Sammy Davis Junior, is fine, chewing grass from the roadside as we go and there are enough pot-holes along the way to keep his thirst at bay. The bad news is that I flung every Snickers at Sinbad in an attempt to get him to the drowning girl faster, resulting in a Snickers-free zone. I need to get them ASAP.

Every now and again, I spot headlights coming up behind us or coming in our direction. Thankfully, the road has no high hedges, but wide grass verges that go right down to a wooded area on both sides. It gives us ample time to trot down the dip and merge with the trees. Not that a single car has passed along this secondary road.

Reader, you might think that it's difficult to hide an elephant, but it's actually not as difficult as it seems, as long as you travel by night and have plenty of trees and hedges should you need to make a run for it. The last thing people are expecting to see is an elephant and they don't see it when it's really there. It brings me to the conclusion that I haven't seen half of what's going on right under my nose. Maybe they *think* they've just seen an elephant, but common sense says no: it's just the morphing shadows. Try it, Reader.

We walk another two hours through a secluded stretch of countryside. Now and again, I feel that I've turned back on myself and not heading southwest as was planned, but I check myself with the stars which appear and disappear as the clouds sail by. As a matter of fact, it's milder, but rain isn't far away.

After another hour or so, I get tired. I want to stop, but we're in the middle of nowhere.

'Maybe it's the best place to stop, Sinbad? Hmm?'

Sinbad traipses along behind me with no intention of answering.

'Uh-huh, not yet then. We'll know when we get there...'

Twenty minutes later, my legs are gone to jelly. I can't go any further. We pull up next to a gate leading into a field and I climb it.

'Sinbad, come.'

Sinbad does as he is asked, sidling up next to me. I've done it once so I'll do it again. Hoping that Sinbad doesn't suddenly take a step to his left, I let myself fall out before landing against Sinbad's mass. I scramble to the top... 'I'm getting too old for this shit...'

I sit myself in between his ears, giggling to myself again, and direct with my heels, just like riding a horse. Sinbad takes to the controls naturally. I'm discovering more about my old friend now than forty years in a cage. I let out another whoop of delight and fist the night sky. I whip out the Canon and take a few selfies for proof, almost blinding myself and falling off with the flash.

From my higher vantage-point, I see the lights of a village below in the distance. I check my watch and see that it's only coming up to 9pm; plenty of time to go and find something to eat. If only I could find somewhere for Sinbad to eat with me:

'Table for two?' I ask in the imaginary waiter's voice.

'Yes, it'll just be myself and the elephant tonight...'

I decide to find a spot where I can safely leave Sinbad, then I can head to the closest shop or supermarket and stock up on provisions, if there is a shop open this late.

We walk another few meters, and as luck would have it, we come across what looks to be an old, disused mill just a few meters off the road.

Oops, now I've got the problem of getting off Sinbad. I hadn't thought about that when I jumped on him. There isn't anything around here that I can use as a step, so I've got no choice but to slide off and hope my ankles can put up with the fall…

So, I slide off Sinbad and the fall seems to take forever, but my ankles *do* hold up as I drop onto the roadside grassy verge.

Sinbad follows me inside. It's dark in here. I switch on my flashlight. Bats flit back and forth through the overhead broken windows.

'Now, Sinbad, I want you to stay here while I go find some grub. You'd fancy a Snickers, I'm sure. Be a good boy and I'll get you one.'

I quickly survey our surroundings and decide it's a good a place as any for Sinbad. There isn't anything that he can harm himself with.

I duck back outside the graffiti-covered building and head for the streetlights a little way down the hill, humming *I Remember When I lost My Mind* – can't remember who the singer is. I'm due a bout of memory-loss any time soon.

I walk along the deserted main street of the village. Just as I'm wondering where I am, I spot a sign reading New Port. New Port is a village just outside Limerick City, I know that much. I *must* be heading in the right direction. I take a selfie with the sign-post in the background and look upwards and thank my lucky stars playing hide-and-go-seek with a cloud-blanket.

I stop outside a little corner-shop that's not on a corner. I check my pocket and discover that my wallet's practically empty!

'Fucking Moron!'

I have my ATM bank card, but no bank!

Oh, mercy!

I have just enough for something simple so I step inside the fine emporium.

There are two women talking to another woman sitting at the cash-till. I join the queue, if that's what you'd call it. I can't help but overhear the following conversation:

Woman Customer A: 'And when did this happen?'

Woman Customer B: 'This evening – just a few hours ago apparently.' Woman Customer B gestures to the street outside as if this, somehow, brings time closer.

Cash-Till Woman: 'Is she okay?' Cash-Till Woman has her hand to her mouth and is blinking profusely.

Woman Customer B: 'A bit shook, but fine. They got to her just in the nick of time.'

Woman Customer A: 'Who? The parents?'

Woman Customer B: Laughs. 'Well, this is where it gets a little *strange*,' putting "strange" in air-commas to make it even stranger. 'The children claim an *elephant* saved the girl.'

Mild gasps of surprise and chuckles while I grow faint.

Woman Customer A: 'Kids and their imaginations.'

Woman Customer B: 'I said the very same to my husband, but the fact is that the parents didn't hear the children screaming for help...so *somebody* or *something* did come to the rescue.'

Woman Customer A: 'Spider Man?'

Woman Customer B: Shrugs her shoulders. 'The thing is this: if it was an elephant, for argument's sake, then somebody must have been with the elephant. Elephants just don't turn up on dairy farms in the middle of the night in Tipperary.' As if elephants *do* turn up in other unmentioned counties. 'Which brings me to my next point: what was that person doing hiding on a farm...and watching children.'

110

Woman Customer A: 'Which brings me to this point: why don't we drop the elephant tom-foolery all together and concentrate on the individual perving on the kids cos *he's* the elephant. Because it's obvious that whoever it was *told* the kids to say it was an elephant who saved the girl.'

The three women are stumped as the plot thickens and mystifies in their heads.

Meanwhile, I'm nauseous and sweating behind them. I can't believe what I'm hearing. The kids spilled the beans! I can't blame them; their parents probably drilled them on what had happened. But it doesn't matter because the story is so outlandish that they prefer to believe the perving paedophile story instead. Sad.

I spot a few pots of noodles on the far shelf…

Woman Customer B: 'Of course, the parents are demanding them to tell the truth, but they're sticking to their elephant story. The parents weren't inclined to believe them until the children provided the evidence…'

Uh-oh.

Woman Customer A: Giggles. 'I can just imagine an elephant going into a telephone box to change into its super-hero costume. What evidence?'

Woman Customer B: 'Talking Tom…'

Woman Customer A and Cash-Till Woman in unison: *'Who?'*

Woman Customer B: 'One of those…*things* kids have on their phones and iThings.' She dismisses it as if it comes from the moon. 'It records voices and plays them back in a funny, um, way.'

Meanwhile Cash-Till Woman suddenly jumps up from behind the counter, bids me a curt 'Hello' and clearly has no interest in hurrying the 'queue' along. She picks up one of today's newspapers and climbs onto her perch.

Meanwhile, Women A and B are growing very curious.

Cash-Till Woman opens the centre pages on the counter. 'And there was me thinking that I'd dreamt the whole thing. Here…' she points to a full-page article. 'This is this evening's paper fresh off the press.' She rubs her thumb along the print and holds it up to the others just to display how fresh the ink is.

I crane my neck to get a peep at the photograph…

And almost pass out when I see, in splendid Technicolor dream-coat, me and Sinbad!

The photograph was taken at the zoo about two years ago during an open-day we had with a few schools from around the country. I'm happy and clean-shaven. And I recall now – how can I forget – that Gloria (my Glow) got the devastating results the following day.

Cash-Till Woman then reads aloud: 'Elephant at Large…'

Woman Customer A: 'They're playing with words…'

Woman Customer B: 'Shush…'

Cash-Till Woman: 'Elephant at Large. Dublin Zoo's oldest elephant, Sinbad, has been kidnapped from the zoo.'

Woman Customer A: *'Kidnapped?!* That should read *escaped.'*

Woman Customer B: 'Shush!'

Cash-Till Woman reads: *'Police are asking people to come forward with information regarding any Indian elephant acting in a suspicious manner in your vicinity.'*

Woman Customer A: 'It's a joke! They're having a laugh with their readers – poking fun at the general public. This newspaper is a rag. Elephants are, by nature, not suspicious – meerkats, now *they're* suspicious. The way they're always standing on their hind feet and gawking at everything that moves – reminds me of my neighbour, Madge. Indian elephant? Hmm, they're stuck in everything. That's the fellah with the big ears.'

Woman Customer B: Not buying into her racism against elephants. *'Small* ears. Shush!'

Cash-Till Woman face-palms the two customers and reads over them as if the article is about to fade away:

'Police are neither confirming nor denying anything, but word on the street is that the elephant didn't work alone. This newspaper's research suggests that a disgruntled, retired elephant-keeper, Mick Munroe, has kidnapped Sinbad because of a previous altercation at the zoo. Dublin Zoo neither confirms nor denies this, though they do admit that they are an elephant short.'

Woman Customer A: 'You can't *kidnap* an elephant…You can *steal* an elephant. But what if you just open its gate? Then, you're an accomplice or what?'

Disgruntled, I think to myself as I back out the door. *Altercation?* At least get the story right.

Without wanting to be recognized, I leave in a flurry of emotions, light a cigarette to calm the nerves, and trot back to the old mill to gather my thoughts.

When I get there I find Sinbad resting; he's feeling the strain too. I can tell.

'We're famous!' I tell Sinbad. 'We're wanted by the police.'

Sinbad doesn't look too fazed.

'I have to get food, Sinbad.' I check my wallet and scrape together enough loose change for one of those pot noodles. 'Then I need to find a Bank ATM ASAP. I'm down to my last fiver. Maybe in the next town…'

Then I find the little origami elephant Gabe had given me. I'd forgotten all about it, but it lifts my heart now to see it.

'I have to go back to the shop, Sinbad. I shouldn't have come back. I should've just gotten the goddamn pot noodle and beat a hasty retreat. Now I've got to go back there acting all suspicious.'

Sinbad nods his head at me.

'Hmm? No, you can't come with me – they'll recognize you, but they might not recognize me; I've let myself go since that photo was taken. I could use a shave and a wash right now. But first thing's first: I need fuel in the engine.'

I wait by Sinbad's side until he nods off like an old man in an armchair. Seeing that he is settled down for the night, I trot back to the shop. A strong wind has begun to blow and it tries to push me back to the mill.

The corner-shop's shutter is half-down. I tap on it. 'Would you mind if I just grabbed something fast? I know what I want.'

The shutter rolls upwards and the same woman ushers me in, looking at my face a moment longer than I care for. I have my trilby pulled down as low over my face as possible without raising suspicion. Will she recognize me?

'Sorry, you caught me yapping earlier on. I noticed you made a run for it…'

Shit. 'I'd forgotten my wallet.'

She nods and smiles. 'Happens every day. What can I get you?'

I quickly scan the shelves and grab a pot of noodles (any flavour) and a litre-bottle of water. I put the loose change on the counter.

While she has her back turned, I quickly fold an issue of the same newspaper she'd read from just half hour previous and slip it inside my coat. I would've asked her, but I didn't want to draw attention.

'Is there a bank in New Port? I don't see any.'

'I'm afraid not. Everybody keeps their money under the mattress.'

I take that as a *No* and duck back under the dropped shutter.

'Oh,' the woman calls, 'keep your eye out for an elephant. There's a loose elephant roaming the country. What next?'

'Is there a reward?' I shout back.

The wind swallows up the woman's answer. But I *know* the answer, Reader. Yes, there probably is a little bounty on our heads. That bounty being the satisfaction that I'm no

114

longer a threat to the public or myself and Sinbad's back behind bars. 'It's for your own good, Mick' I hear them say.

I walk away from the shop with my noodles and newspaper, but instantly feel guilty for having stolen the newspaper. I've never stolen anything in my life, but I guess this sort of fits in with my new on-the-run status. The number one rule if you're ever a fugitive, Reader: never give them an opportunity to suspect anything.

By now, there's a storm gale whistling through the streets. But I'm happy I've got my much-coveted noodles…

Wait… How could I be so stupid?! '*Fucking* moron!' I curse myself.

I've got the *Pot Noodle*, but I don't have a microwave. 'Now what?!' I ask myself.

Down at the other end of the street, I see a Guinness sign and that means there's a pub. They might let me heat it up there…but that means explaining why I've got a Pot Noodle in a storm without a microwave.

I have a plan…

Not able to think of a better reason not to spend the last of my money, I wade into the wind, never losing sight of that glowing pint of Guinness.

I go inside. It's a typical local for locals, nothing fancy, with deco stuck in the 80's. I approach the woman behind the counter. She is a large, chirpy woman with a head of blonde hair cut short and a shock of hot-pink fringe to offset her normalness, which kind of suits her.

I ask her for a pint of Guinness to appear normal…that's my plan, Reader. Okay, so it's no master plan, but I blend in and that's what counts. By blending in, one asks for Guinness. Then I hit her with the big one: 'Oh, I almost forgot, any chance of heating this up for me?' I try to sound casual as I slide the *Pot Noodle* cross the counter.

This gets everybody's attention. It's like something out

of the Wild West.

The woman smiles. 'Noodles? You must be stuck.'

'That's one way of putting it…'

She smiles. 'I'll heat this up for you.' She titters to herself and walks off, finds her glasses, and starts reading the cooking instructions.

I thank her and take a seat to myself and savour the Guinness – I don't know when or where my next pint will be.

She comes back a few minutes later and hands me my piping-hot noodles.

All eyes on me as I spoon in the first mouthful.

'Lordy, but there's nothing like a pot of noodles on a night like this,' observes a customer as I tuck into the noodles and wash them down with my pint.

The old boy next to him swivels on his stool and looks down the counter at me with one wall-eye. 'Hmm, oh boy. What flavour, sir?'

'Uhm…' I'm so hungry I don't know what flavour it is. 'Noodle,' I answer back, gobbling down the pot's contents.

The old boy skits and scratches the peak cap on his head. 'I see where you're comin' from.'

I finish the goddamn noodles as lithely as possible and down the second half of my pint in one, then get the hell out of the pub. I never knew noodles would attract so much attention. I should have known better, Reader. But I suppose I can be thankful that all the attention was on the noodles and not on the stranger eating them.

The rain is vicious when I step outside; *angry* rain, Reader, angry. I raise my collar as far as it will go, batten down my trilby, and face into the storm. But the real storm is about to kick off because, when I get back, Sinbad is nowhere to be seen.

I swear at myself with all my heart. '*Fucking* moron!'

I *must* be a moron tonight, Reader. Sorry for the expletives, but I must be stupid to go drinking a pint while my elephant was free to wander. I should've just heated up the noodles and come back. There are no doors on this draughty, old carcass of a building. My belly had gotten the better of me. And that's not the worst of it: in my greediness, I've forgotten Sinbad's chocolate. Oh, mercy…

'Sinbad? *Sorry!* I shouldn't have left you on your own. Where are you?'

I run back outside and call into the screaming wind: 'Sinbad!?' I swear, spit, and curse to the high Heavens. *'Sinbaaad!'* Feeling horribly guilty, I run off into the wood that surrounds the old mill and look along the river that's coming dangerously close to its banks. *'Sinbaaad? Where are you?!'* I wander off further into the woods, until it gets so dense that I can hardly see anything now.

Oops, I'm a little lost… I should've left a trail of bread crumbs, but I didn't have the gumption nor the bread. I walk around in circles…

Suddenly, I see car headlights off in the distance, fractured through swaying trees. I follow them, inching forwards every few feet into the oncoming gale and poking branches. I've forgotten about finding Sinbad, but finding my whereabouts instead. I follow the beaming lights, but they seem to be at an odd angle, shining off into the woods, and the car is stopped. I *know* that stretch of secondary road, and there isn't any reason why a car should be stopped there…

Then a horrible image comes to me. Please, don't let Sinbad be involved. I pick up into a run, fully convinced that a car has crashed into Sinbad. I burst my way through the undergrowth, slashed and scratched, but panic is chasing me down like a ghost in the woods.

I come out into an opening, which I quickly gather is the road itself. As I close in, squinting my eyes from the rain, I see that a large tree has fallen right through the roof a brand new 4x4 flame-red Mazda. The Mazda's engine is still running, raindrops turn to steam on the headlamps. It must have just happened. The bonnet has crumpled beneath the main trunk of the tree and one of the two main lower branches is inside the car and the windshield has caved inwards. I'm ashamed to say that I'm almost relieved; it would have ended my world on this stormy night if Sinbad had been –

'Help! Help me!'

I freeze.

'Help me!' comes the yell again, barely audible in the wind. I pluck up the courage to peer into the car and see a woman sitting in the driver's seat, covered in horror-movie blood. She keeps moaning in low, painful sobs. 'I can't move…I can't…'

The tree branch has pinned her in. I don't know what to do. The authorities are going to be on the scene in a minute and find me – *us* – wherever my *fucking* elephant has gone! What a mess!

Stupidly, I try and lift the tree and I curse myself for doing a Bean impression. I think this is my second impression on this journey of self-discovery.

'Did you ring anybody?'

'I can't get to my phone! I think I've broken my collar-bone…'

I reach for my phone, but stall before I ring. They can trace calls. They'll find me and take away my elephant – if he's not gone already. They'll put us both behind bars. 'Sorry, I don't have a phone.' I switch off mine completely to avoid being followed by satellites and save some battery. 'Where is yours?' I feel terrible for lying under such circumstances…

The woman has hardly any energy to speak. She nods to the dash and I see the phone in a holder. Luckily, it appears intact. In the back of my mind, I'm grateful I don't have to go sifting through her blood-soaked clothes. I don't know if I'll ever meet another woman, but please, not under these circumstances. I pull my trilby's peak down over my eyes so that she won't be able to identify me, reach in, take the phone from its cradle, and dial 999. I quickly deduct that the woman is lodged between two branches, but they're not weighing on her. She has the luck of the gods on her side tonight. If she'd moved six inches left or right, this tree would've split her down the middle. I quickly inform the woman on the other end of the line of the situation. She tells me that there's going to be a delay because all units are out dealing with emergencies due to the storm.

'But this woman is bleeding to death!'

'We're *doing* all we can. Please, can you give me your name and location?'

Pause. 'Um, we are on the outskirts of New Port – not sure exactly where. A secondary road… There's an old mill next to us.'

'And your name is?'

'What does it matter what my name is.' I hang up and place the phone on the dash and tell her that help is on its way, but I don't mention when it will arrive.

Suddenly, my sixth sense kicks in. I feel I'm being watched. I turn around from the smashed Mazda and something grabs me by the face. I scream, embarrassingly like a little girl. An enormous dark shadow, silhouetted against the sky is standing right behind me. It's like something out of Doom's Day…

Or is it?

'Sinbad?' My elephant is standing there on the road. 'Sinbad!' His trunk (which I thought had been an alien's tentacle) checks me out. My old friend is back again! I'm suddenly torn between running to give him a hug and staying with the stricken woman…

'Wait!' I look at Sinbad again. 'I have an idea, Sinbad…'

You thinking what I'm thinking, Reader?

I've done it before, so why not again?

I beckon my elephant forward.

'Here, Sinbad, here!' I slap the trunk of the tree, but Sinbad's got *his* trunk in my pocket, searching for a much coveted chocolate bar.

The woman moans in pain… '*Pleeease*, help! Who's Sinbad? Hello?' Now, there's fear in the woman's voice. 'Who are yoooou?'

'*Fucking moron!!!*' Now she knows his name! How many locals in the southwest of Ireland are called Sinbad?! I should've just stuck with Sammy Davis Junior.

The car is facing forward so, thank Christ, she cannot see what's going on behind her.

I get nervous and start pushing the tree to show Sinbad what to do… '*Push, Sinbad! Push!*'

Sinbad takes this as his cue. He triple tapers his trunk around the tree trunk and heaves…and I heave with him, Reader, heaving so hard that I grow dizzy. I have forgotten that I'm an old man…And that's the best thing about this crazy journey: I am forgetting that I'm an old man instead of the Alzheimer's reminding me by forgetting. Do you get it, Reader? Maybe I didn't explain myself very well, but there are other forces at hand right now…

Sinbad loses grip of the tree and drops it a little…

The woman screams…

'Up, Sinbad! Up!!! Up!!' I wave my arms upwards in great big waving arcs so my elephant can see.

He lifts the thick branch in one almighty heave, backs up, and angles the tree over the totalled Mazda in one drag and drops it at the side of the road.

'Good! Good boy!'

I check the woman and see that she's got room to move now.

'Thank you! Thank you!' The woman is crying, sobbing like a baby. 'How did you…I mean, how did you lift the tree? *Who* is Sinbad? Please tell me? He just saved my life… My name is Rebecca! Thank you!'

'You're going to be okay now.' *Those scars will last*

120

forever, but who doesn't have scars? Some have them on
the outside and others have them on the inside…

I reach into the car, amongst the twisted metal and glass
shards, and assure her that everything is going to be okay.
She'll need to be cut out. There's no point asking Sinbad as
he'll only drag the car from one side of the road to the next.

I kiss her on the head, I don't know why, but a strange
feeling just came over me; I feel like her protector.

She asks me for a cigarette and I give her one, lighting it
first. 'If a tree won't kill you, these will…'

She smiles weakly. 'There's always something, right?'

Off in the distance, I hear the wail of approaching sirens
and decide to bail. I beckon Sinbad and he follows. I duck
down into the undergrowth of the woods, going in far
enough so that Sinbad won't be seen from the road. I watch
over the woman until the ambulance pulls up. I hear
talking, but the words are lost to the screaming wind. I
think I hear 'Sinbad…' in that conversation, but the wind is
playing with my imagination.

We back-track along an old path until we come out into
an open field that is thrown into intermittent silver glow
and darkness as the clouds pass under the full moon. As we
walk, I feel an intensity that I've never felt before, not even
as a teenager when most experiences are new. I've gone
beyond that and into the realm of the ridiculously sublime.
I look upwards and thank my lucky stars. They wink back
down at me every time they show their faces beyond the
racing clouds. I hear the ambulance sirens moving off into
the distance.

I'm not a religious man, Reader, but if you told me that
Sinbad and I were chosen by a higher being to do good,
then I might believe you 'round about now. If you told me
that *chance* has chosen us to do good, then I'd *definitely*
believe you. Whatever way you look at it, Reader, we seem
to have found our calling.

I'm just about to label myself a saviour, not *the* saviour, but just *a* saviour, when the ground swallows me up…

A Chapter I'd Rather Forget

I am suddenly and irrefutably humbled by a complete lack of memory as the mind-thief, Alzheimer's, sneaks up on me and pounces, just as my elephant and I had become saviours.

I come to a stop in the middle of this field. Where am I going? More importantly, where am I coming from? I'm all alone. But I'm not panicking because this isn't the first time that I find myself lost… I've got this strange déjà vu that I cannot shake.

I fall to the grass and curl up like a foetus, forgetting that I was Earth's saviour just minutes ago. Standing over me is an elephant. *An elephant?!* Am I dreaming? OMG and WTF as the youngsters say nowadays.

I clamber to my feet and bolt (a 60 yr-old bolt) from the elephant, but the elephant follows me… I run, stumble, and fall to the wet grass. I know something is wrong, but I can't remember what it *is* that's wrong. The elephant is standing over me again, insisting it doesn't leave my side and careful not to stand on me, and now caressing me with its trunk. It seems to worry about me. The animal's trunk wraps itself around my shoulder and arm-pit and pulls me up to my feet as if I were a rag-doll. The trunk nudges me forwards…

I begin to walk, but stop dead in my tracks…

There's somebody standing just up ahead, right in the middle of the field, on this dark, stormy night. The fact that there is somebody standing in the middle of a field, on a stormy night, doesn't seem to bother me. I need to speak to somebody. Maybe they can tell me where I'm going and why I've got an Indian elephant playing tag with me.

I snatch my flashlight from my backpack and wave it at the stranger. I can see the silhouette of the person standing still, *too* still, maybe twenty meters ahead. 'Excuse me, hello! I am lost.' This is an understatement. 'I seem to have wandered off the road a way back and I've acquired, um, this elephant. I don't know how and, um…'

I come up on the individual and shine the flashlight in the distorted sack-face, on a head bloated with straw. To my dismay, I've just walked up on a scarecrow. He's wearing a straw bonnet and a long, ragged trench-coat. Inside the ankle-length coat, he's got a black and red flannel shirt and what look like pyjama-bottoms for trousers. He's even got an old, worn pair of *Dr. Marten* boots. I hold the flashlight up closer to his wizened, weather-beaten face. Time has blinded and deafened him, and robbed him of a smile. The changing of the seasons has lent him the look of a Celtic pagan God who has watched over this patch of land long before any farmer claimed it as his own. But the scarecrow-king knows that he *is* the land. I look up at him, arms outstretched on a wooden cross. He could be...well, I think you know who he could be, Reader.

Call it dementia … romanticism … desperation … senility … loneliness … a cocktail of all of the above, but I feel protected by this individual and I fall at his feet and ask him to guide me. Now, I know who the *real* saviour is.

Exhausted, I let sleep take me and let planet Earth go to Hell.

The Devil and His Hell Monster

I wake at the Dr. Marten-clad feet of a scarecrow.

'How have I ended up here?' I ask the scarecrow, but the scarecrow remains tight-lipped, observing the land.

'Uh-huh. You see, Mr. Scarecrow, if you're familiar with Newton's third law, then you'll probably know that: *For every action, there is an equal and opposite reaction.* So, taking this into account, sorry, this is getting technical, if I had temporary memory-loss just a few hours ago, then I wouldn't have known how I ended up here or what I had been doing to end up here. If I keep going at this rate I won't know whether I'm coming or going.'

My journey southwest is more precarious than I'd first thought. How can I put this into perspective for you, dear Reader: I feel like I am riding my elephant while he walks across a tight-rope while both ends of the rope are fizzling and fading as my memory crumbles. All I need is a few lucid nights and days to get me down to the Great Blasket Islands and there we will live in peace and harmony and I will camp out in the derelict ruins that once belonged to the Great Blasket writers. I have read Peg Seyers and Tomas Crohan and the childhood land they painted is where I want to be. They were part of Ireland, but also living on their own island away from the rest, which was tough magic. There, let the wild Atlantic whisk my memory away on its waves.

I look up at the scarecrow on his cross. 'It's just a plan. I need to get from A to B and B is for Blaskets – B is my Valhalla. Does it exist? Who knows? But what I *do* know is that if I don't have a B, then I won't know when to stop and maybe I'll be circling the planet for the rest of my days until eucalyptus trees begin to look familiar in The Outback and gorse bushes in Ireland take on a familiarity and Elvis marriage-chapels in Las Vegas become distinguishable.'

'Fair enough.' Getting no joy from the scarecrow, I stand

up slowly to stop the rush of blood to the head that I've been getting recently. I look to the four corners of this field. Sinbad, to my relief, is over in the furthest corner. Looks like he's found something tasty in the branches of a horse-chestnut tree.

For the rest of the day, we stick around the field. I'm starving, but there's nothing I can do without the cloak of darkness...

'What if this whole adventure ends by me losing my memory and walking up to the authorities with Sinbad following behind? I cannot think of a worse way to end this, but it *is* a strong possibility right now.'

The scarecrow gives me the impression, by telepathic ventriloquism, that there are worse things in life.

'True. I should be happy having gotten this far. How have I managed to escape with a 4-tonne elephant? You're absolutely correct, anything from here on in is just a bonus. It's all been worth it and if the authorities close in around us now, then I'll go to the gallows a happy camper.'

Just after dusk, about 5.30pm in the evening, we rise with the bats. I say goodbye to my new friend, the scarecrow. I'd gotten to know him quite well, having nobody else to talk to when Sinbad was off foraging. I got a lot off my chest actually. I hope I will see the scarecrow again someday. He's a great listener and it's nice to think of him on his cross, gazing out across the land, with my secrets and the secrets of any other traveller who happens to need a shoulder to cry on; though don't lean too hard on that shoulder as it's made of straw and don't press him for answers should you come across him.

I take a selfie with the scarecrow. 'Cheese!' Just another photo to add to my photo-journal. I will use it to jog my memory when my forgetful bouts become daily missing events in my life. The scarecrow has weightier thoughts on his straw mind and doesn't smile for the camera. I don't blame him; it would be a step down from his reverie. He's just like a Buckingham Guard, but wears the fluffy stuff inside his head instead of outside it.

I need sustenance. I don't have a lot of energy, so I climb aboard Sinbad and kick him in a southwest direction according to the stars. You've probably gathered by now that my itinerary (Smiler would turn in his grave if he were dead) is a little scattergun because we travel as the crow flies. But the constellations in the night sky do keep me on-track, Reader.

We leave New Port, Tipperary, and take to the by-roads of South West Ireland, secretly thanking whoever is looking down on me – maybe Gloria – for the sparse population in this neck of the woods. I do believe she is watching over me and my crazy capers. I can just hear her now:

Mick Munroe, what has gotten into you? You're acting like a common delinquent!

Everything was "common" with my Glow.

In just a couple of hours, I see the orange night-time glow of a city, which can only be Limerick City, which tells me that we crossed over the Tipperary border and into Limerick somewhere back there. The night-sky orange-pink glow also means too many eyeballs, so we circumnavigate (that's a word Smiler might use). So we do.

But now I have a predicament. I've never been so hungry in my life while Sinbad has a constant stream of fresh grass to pick at. I cannot, for obvious reasons, drift into the city with an Indian elephant; that might draw unwanted attention. *That* would be a Sinbad Show…No, better again, *Sinbad on Ice*… I don't think I'm going to find a village big enough to have an ATM machine or a bank of any description, nor can I enter the city. I have no choice but to knock on a door and beg for food. Oh, mercy,

Reader! I'll have to play the wanderer living off the goodness of others. I'll play the pilgrim, though I'm not on any pilgrimage.

I feel like this is getting a little out of hand.

We make a wide berth east of the city and head west, skipping any terraced houses. What I need to find is a house out on its own, surrounded by lots of vegetation and with room for an elephant (to hide one, at least). We skirt along the M20 motorway, staying far into the fields not to be spotted by any driver's headlights. And there *are* an amazing amount of drivers travelling the roads at night, mainly truckers.

I cannot go on. 'Down, Sinbad.' Surprisingly, Sinbad does as I ask and I climb aboard. I should've done this the first time instead of the zoo manager walking in on me in mid-air.

Just when I'm about to fall asleep to the gentle rocking of Sinbad, we come to a large, old country home. There's a black Volkswagen van parked up outside that's strangely at odds with the regal-looking homestead. Don't ask me why, just a gut reaction.

I park up Sinbad out of sight, and slide/fall off him. Like a soldier, I've mastered my fall. It's only a matter of time before Sinbad gets cranky without his Snickers and, Reader, you don't want to be around Sinbad when he's cranky.

I knock on the front door, quickly running over my line that I will spout when the door opens. *'Sorry to be calling at your door at such an hour, but I was wondering if you could spare some food? I don't want any money. I just need food to get me to the next town where I can withdraw money. I left my money at home and all I have is my ATM card...'* That's when the door shuts in my face...

Only there's no answer...

I was sure I'd seen light coming from inside, but would I open my door at this ungodly hour? No sir. Would you,

Reader? I knock again for good measure because things always happen in threes, that's what my old man used to say. And I think, for the most part, he might be right.

I hear movement just inside the front door; I can almost imagine somebody peering out at me through the fisheye. I knock again and immediately put my ear to the wood and listen hard, even squeezing my eyes shut as if this will somehow heighten my hearing. I hear mumbling coming from inside the hallway and somebody telling somebody else to "'Sshh!'" and "'Shut the *fuck* up!'"

None of this tallies. I've stumbled on something here...Maybe I should just turn and leave, but I'm a new man since I hit the road and nothing fazes me. I speak through the letter-box. 'Sorry, no cause for alarm. I'm not a burglar.' I laugh stupidly at my own joke and clear my throat. 'I was wondering if you could spare something – *anything* – to eat. I'm on foot...' *a lie...* 'and have no money till I find a bank. Only something to eat – pass it through the letter-box, a few slices of bread or something; perfect size.' I don't know why I have to put my fingers through the letter-box to show the dimensions, but I do...

...and *scream* as somebody on the other side of the door smashes them.

I draw my throbbing hand back and see that my knuckles are raw and bleeding.

'Fine! I'm sorry I asked for a measly slice of bread! This country!'

I stomp away down the lane, cursing the backward yokels of the country-house before I double back by the paddock leading off the house. I bring Sinbad with me, coaxing him with one of the mini Snickers wrappers I squirreled away for a rainy day. He's going to get pissed off real soon when he realizes that they're just wrappers.

I hide in the bushes and wait, never losing sight of the front door of the house.

Just as I'm about to give up hope that the door will ever open, it clicks and opens a crack. Somebody sticks their face out, ghostly in the moonlight, and disappears inside again before the door opens wide. I witness three men stride cross the road, from the house to the van with the *contents* of the house, including the wailing cat.

I've just stumbled on a robbery… Oh, mercy! Here we go again. Why me?

In my confusion, I take out my Canon and begin to take snaps of everything…the house…the van…the van's plates. Yes, very good, but they're still in there. What do I do *now,* Reader? Confront them? I don't think so. Looking at my knuckles, God only knows what they might do to the rest of me. I could confront them with Sinbad, but then what? There would either be casualties or they'd drive off…or both. I can't ring the police because they'll have my number.

I take my old Nokia and go to punch in Smiler's number because he can ring from his phone. But I can't remember his number. I've *never* forgotten his number, Reader. I never use the call log, but I do it now and see names, but to my utter horror, *they* look confusing too. I can see the names, but cannot figure them out. It is like living in a dream where the absurd is possible. This is another phase of my Alzheimer's I have never seen. End Game is coming, Reader. If nothing else happens, I know I will forget myself out of existence as I climb the seven steps to Alzheimer's Heaven. The doctors tell me that I'm a stage three and have all the hallmarks of reaching stage four with moderate to severe deterioration. My life-altering illness has brought me here in the first place. Without the illness, I would never have had this life-altering journey – and it *is* a journey on so many levels.

Sorry, I'm waffling again. Just give me a little kick under the table. That's it, reach your foot across and nudge mine. Tell me that I'm beginning to dodder and wander. I need to know, just don't play along with me, Reader. Just sit me down, shut me up, and tell me to listen. Those poor old bastards in nursing homes don't know what planet they're living on. Sure, Alzheimer's does that, but nurse, do you have to play along and pretend that everything is Disneyland?

The robbers duck back inside the house and appear with more objects for the van…

I can't make sense of the numbers or names on my phone, but I *am* thinking clearly on the rest…And that's what I find about my illness. It attacks one place at a time and leaves the other intact. I know everything will fall at the end, so I need to use the parts that are working. What I decide to do, Reader, is plain stupid, but like I said, I'm in too deep. Blame it on the slice of bread! If they had just handed over the bread everything would've been fine and they could've gotten on with their robbery. But no. They have crossed Mick Munroe with a sliced pan and, by Christ, every time they reach for their toasters they'll think of me.

'Come, Sinbad…' I command, keeping my voice to a strained whisper.

Sinbad's hulking mass looms across the road. Without much of a hurry, he wades across the road and up to the door of the house to meet me. My heart is thumping in my chest and temples. It's all over if anybody happens to drive past right now. What would they think?

We wait outside for the robbers…

Too late to turn back now. What would Gloria say?

That thought fizzles away when the front door opens and three unsavoury individuals freeze with hot domestic appliances in their clutches. The shock of what they think they see is enough to make them drop their loot, just to show how hot they are.

It all happens in seconds…

'What the fuck's that?!' screams one of the robbers

when they see the monstrous outline of Sinbad behind me…

I realize that I'm still holding my camera. Without thinking, I seize the moment, swerve around and snap a selfie. The flash lights up in the confused and shocked villains' faces. Another nugget for the memory bank I've been building up for that day I no longer remember. Will I recognize myself in the photos and remember these 'special moments' or will it be like looking at a stranger. Does it matter? I mean, does it really matter? Just savour the moment. Even taking the goddamn selfie is unforgettable! I can't believe what I've just done! Can't wait to see their horrified expressions in the selfie…

The thieves slam the door shut and quickly lock it.

Now what?! I've got the rats trapped but rats find holes, and if they don't, they gnaw their way out.

As if these shocks to the system rattle my clogged mind, everything is clear again; the hazy cloud of forgetfulness has sailed away for now. Like a flash from the heavens, I perform an old trick that Smiler had once taught me: how to hide Caller ID. I punch in the 'hide caller ID' number and dial 999 for the second time in just a few hours.

'Hello.'

'Hello, sir. My name is Shannon. How can I help you?'

'I need the police…fast! I've got…'

The door jars on my shoulder as the robbers kick and pound at it. I order Sinbad to 'Push!' and slap at the door for him to see. He shoves his trunk against the door and almost drives the door-frame in on itself.

'I've got three, maybe four robbers cornered in a house.'

'Can you give me your whereabouts, sir?'

'I'm in the middle of nowhere.'

'Could you be more specific?'

'I'm just outside the village of Adare. It's a big country house.'

'Sir, I'm going to contact the local police in that area and they might know where you are. What's the nature of the call?'

'The *nature* of the call? It's an *emergency!*'

'Yes, sir, I'm aware that it's an emergency.'

'Look, could we side-line the pleasantries for later? Hmm? Maybe we'll have a drink some time and we can talk all about it.'

In a sharper tone, she asks, 'Why are you ringing the emergency service, sir?'

I scream *fucking moron* silently at my phone. '*Again?!* Look, I've trapped some burglars I happened to stumble upon while they were robbing a house. I don't know the owner of the house. I'm not from around here. They wouldn't pass the sliced pan through the letter-box so I…'

'Sliced pan through the letter-box? Please don't waste our valuable time by –'

'Look, it's a long story. But I'm genuine. I'm *telling* the truth!'

'So what were you doing in the vicinity of the house at this hour of the night?'

'Look, this isn't an Agatha Christie whodunit! It's a long story. *Puh-leeease*, just get the police over here. I don't know how much longer I can hold them…' *Though Sinbad isn't under any pressure…*

'Wait, what do you mean when you say you're "holding them"?'

Oh, mercy. '*Yes*, I've trapped them in the house.' *My kidnapped elephant named Sinbad, you might've seen him in the newspapers, has jammed his trunk against the door…*

There's a pause down the line. '*Hellooo?*'

'Okay, sir. Try to remain calm.'

'Remaining calm is on my agenda, yes, but you're making it difficult.'

'I'm only doing my job. The police are on their way. They think they know the house.'

'They think??'

One of the robbers' boots comes through the door. It shatters down the middle, sending me sideways and landing on my side on the tarmac. One of the robbers peers through the cracked door like a devilish imp and all I can think is, *'Heeere's Jooohnny!'*

By some kind of divine intervention, Sinbad is startled by the splinter of timber. His wild, inner nature kicks in. He rears up on his two back legs – something I've never seen before – and he growls and blares at the robbers, flapping his ears.

The thieves are just as startled as Sinbad is. The Devil himself and his Hell Monster pet are keeping them captive inside the house.

The face disappears from the hole in the door, and the bunch of thieves run back inside the house like a bunch of kids screaming and shouting in a language foreign to me. One of them even tries to pull the smashed door back into its frame behind them. They scamper down the hallway and lock themselves into another room. I see them through what's left of the same letter-box I'd asked for bread earlier.

I hear sirens (something I'm getting used to, Reader) rolling in from the distance. I've come to learn that the siren call is my call to duck low, so I call Sinbad. 'Come!'

But Sinbad is getting tired of my mono-syllable commands. I call him again, but he wants to get caught at the scene of the crime. I curse to the stars and rustle in my pockets till I find a Snickers wrapper. And as I have fooled my old friend so many times on this journey, I fool him once again. I feel guilty for it, but it's for the best. When this whole thing is done and dusted, I'm going to treat Sinbad to a few family packs. It'll probably be his last supper.

I run away down the road with my elephant running behind me, still a little prickly. For such a big animal, elephants can pick up a lot of speed and Sinbad could outrun me if he wanted. I find a fence and scramble along it till I find a gate to open for Sinbad. I try to open it, but it's locked. I become frantic with panic, attempting to get the gate open to let my elephant through, but it's shut tight. I try to get Sinbad as close up to the gate as possible so he won't be spotted by the police when their lights hit the straight of this country road.

Through the bushes, I see two squad cars pull up outside the house. The police are too busy to notice the elephant just a little way down the road, trying to hide, but with his enormous butt half way out on the road. I've said it before and I'll say it again: it's amazing what the eyes overlook when something's not on the agenda.

I've seen enough to know that the robbers are in good hands. We trot along the road while the police are engaged and duck down a passageway with Sinbad following behind.

Tonight, we fall asleep hungry (me, at least). I *need* to find an ATM *fast* and get some money to stock up on provisions. I never thought when I set out on this adventure, that hunger would prove my greatest enemy.

I sleep in an outhouse – a sheep outhouse, to be more exact. Hundreds of stark, oblong pupils stare into the beam of my flashlight, bleating and baaing every time something moves. They have sheep-bells hanging from their necks and they constantly clang as I pen my escapades in this journal. It's so cold tonight that the ink keeps drying up and the pen itself has frozen in my numb fingers. I threaten the onlookers that I will steal one of their woollen coats. I'm only joking about the coat, but this cacophony of pealing bells gives me an idea…

I climb into the sheep pen. Sheep scatter in all directions. I didn't know sheep could jump so high. I corner one, but he gets away. I corner another, and wrangle him to the ground. I quite fancy mutton tonight, but it's the bell I'm after. I undo the bell-collar and go outside to Sinbad and tie the bell onto his tail. Sinbad doesn't like the idea of a bell strapped to his behind (would you?), but I cannot run any more risks. He tries to shake it free from his stubby tail, but I tighten it securely.

'At least I'll be able to track you if you go missing again.'

It's midnight. I set my digital watch (relic Casio) for three hours from now.

'That will give us enough sleep and enough time to move on and get a little closer to our destination.'

I find it difficult to sleep after my adrenaline-high, so I resort to counting sheep.

Forget-Me-Nots

At three a.m., 16th March, we take to the byways once again, heading southwest. Sinbad's sheep-bell clangs back and forth and it puts me at ease for some reason. The knock of the clapper sets a rhythm going. I feel I'm on a mission, Reader. I won't say a Saviour Mission because I've already been humbled by that, but there's something at work here. Even you have to admit that…

It is very dark tonight, Reader, and for the first time I rely on my flashlight. My lucky stars are hiding tonight. I have never felt hunger like now. All I am eating is my medication and washing it down with water which comes in plentiful supply in the potholes of these secondary roads and paths; I finished the bottle of water long ago. I should've bought more, but at the time, I was a little nervy after seeing my on-the-run self in the newspaper. I'm not prepared, in other words. But then again, this trip was never really on any itinerary of mine. Sometimes, I think that I should've just gone to visit Sinbad that night, and left it at that. My life would be much simpler, but sadder and without direction. Now, I have direction: southwest.

Reader, five minutes ago, I passed a sign reading Old Castle in County Limerick, not far from the border with County Kerry where my destination lies. As per custom, I take a selfie with the road-sign in the background. I check to see the image I captured, and I laugh to myself on seeing Sinbad's wandering trunk photo-bomb, as the youngsters say nowadays.

Old Castle is a sizable town, if the outskirts are anything to go by. I've heard of this town before, only God knows why, but the place is dead to the world tonight. Not that I'm actually in the town itself, but skirting around it as normal.

Just as the rain begins to fall, we come across a rather

substantial park. I let Sinbad roam at will in a field of sizable proportions, and I still get the same kick I got when we started out on this journey, seeing him discover new things, like a kid. I find shelter in some stands overlooking the field. There is a little stream across the way and Sinbad has gravitated towards that. I'm hungry and have no food, but I *do* have my ATM bank card...and I know there will be an ATM in this town. Hallelujah.

I take a big chance by leaving Sinbad here while I go and look for a bank. You'd think that I might've learned a lesson from the last time. I've no choice; there isn't anywhere to house him. Sinbad loves to play in water, and I think the stream will buy me enough time to get back. And if he strays then the sound of his bell will guide me.

I follow a direct route through a short-cut that runs along the wall of a water-bottling plant that leads me right into the town square.

To my delight, there are three banks right here! Not one, but three! Bank of Ireland, Allied Irish Bank, and the Permanent TSB. It's the last one I'm interested in, so I cross the town square. A black cat runs out from under a car in front of me, scaring me shitless. Apart from the cat and my resulting gulp, there's nothing stirring in town and I must admit that I'm beginning to appreciate the ghostly beauty of towns and villages in the dead hour. It's a side of life we rarely see.

I approach the bank and I'm suddenly wondering why I'm approaching the bank? What had I been doing beforehand?

I can't remember...

I'm so frustrated with myself. I swear and slap myself up around the side of my head. *'Fucking moron!'*

I look around me...

Out of the blue, I suddenly have no idea where I am. I can't remember which way I came to the bank. I look at the lit town square and see streets leading off in all four directions, even a fifth leading up a side-street. To my right

I see a castle with a horse and rider outside it made of bronze-turned-green. Across the way, I see an all-night chipper and some closed shops. But none of it makes any sense to me. What was I doing to get here? Why am I here? My old man always told me to retrace my steps, but what's the point of that if I can't remember where my feet are, let alone my footsteps…

Scratching my head whilst trying to look as if I know what I'm doing, I wander around the square a few times, waiting for my memory to catch up, but nothing comes. I read the street names on the building corners to see if that will help, but no spark there either.

I cross to the centre of the square which is a raised cobblestone area. I sit against the granite pedestal of a stone cross, light up a cigarette, and wait for this terrifying wave to pass. Reader, it's scary and it's not. I know it'll pass, but while I'm in this state, the world has no past or future.

Terrified, I call the first number I see on my phone and listen to the dial tone wondering who I am ringing. My gut tells me that I shouldn't be doing this, but I don't know why.

'Hello?'

'Mick, where are you?'

'Who?'

'Are you okay, Mick?'

I can't place the voice. I can see the name flashing in bright neon in the air in front of me, but the image is fuzzy and can't make it out. I try to reach out to draw it in closer, but the further I reach, the further back the neon name recedes.

'Sorry, who am I speaking to?'

There was a pause on the line. 'This is Smiler, Mick. Is everything okay? The police are looking for you. I should've rang. Where are you?'

'I don't know.'

'Mick, the elephant? Where's Sinbad?'

I begin to cry. *'I don't know!! I don't know anything!! What Elephant?!'*

'Jesus, Mick. Where *are* you?! I'm coming to get you. Stay right where you are. If I leave now, I'll be with you in…three hours. You have to come home and get some treatment. But I can't come to find you until you tell me where you are. Describe what you see?'

I tell him about the castle and the green bronze statue of a knight on a horse in front of it.

'That could be *anywhere*, Mick. Gimme street names. Look for a street name.'

I go back down the street a little. 'Bishop Street…'

Sighs come down the line and into my left ear. 'Don't know…'

'I'm not coming home, um…'

'Smiler…'

'Smiler, I'm not coming home because my elephant needs me. Treatment for what, anyway? I feel fine. Hungry, but fine.'

Another pause. 'The Alzheimer's, Mick. So you *do* remember your elephant?'

I do, Reader, *now* I do! I hadn't realized that Sinbad had gone and come back to my memory. The memory-fail sneaks in and out without me knowing. Suddenly, it all comes gushing back to me: I focus in on the neon name: Smiler! I'm in Old Castle! Now what? I know I'm only looking for trouble by bringing him here. 'Smiler, I shouldn't have rang. I just couldn't remember.'

'Jesus, Mick, the police are looking for you. They're treating it as theft and so is the zoo. Long is trying to get you off the hook, pleading that you're insane, but it's not working. Devious Deirdre and Co. have gotten the Health Board involved, and their top shrinks say that what you're doing is pre-determined and nothing to do with your illness. So they've got a bounty on your head, Mick.'

There's a pause. 'They're probably tracking this call right now.'

I'm not sure if Smiler is taking the piss or is serious.

He comes back on the line. 'But you are insane! Shit-crazy insane. I'm kind of jealous…'

'Sorry for everything.' I pause. 'Wait, I think I remember where I am! I'm in –'

For a second, I think that I've hung up on Smiler, but my phone has just died. Battery. I almost gave in just then, but the phone died before I could give Smiler my whereabouts. What are the chances, Reader? Somebody *is* watching over me. Okay, that's it. No more weakness. I *have* to keep us hidden – as hidden as my disease was before I finally told anybody. That much, Reader, I have clear. Being found means I will die, in every way except actual death itself. Drama Queen? Right now, I don't think so. If I'm caught, Sinbad will be sent back to the zoo to be abused, and I'll be banned from visiting him. The only visiting will be done by friends – visiting me in prison or most probably a residence for people like me who can no longer remember who they are and wear nappies all day. Either way, I'm a dodo in the doo-doo. How can I give up on all that now when I feel alive for the first time in a long time?

I come to my senses, but the world is murky. I'm worsening. I know this because the world (*my* world) isn't as crisp as it used to be after an idle bout of forgetfulness. The effects of the Alzheimer's are beginning to linger as my brain shrinks. I thought I would be oblivious to this (the docs told me I would go largely in ignorance for the first couple of years), but I do see myself sinking. If the doctors hadn't confirmed the illness, I'd still know that there was something not right inside. The only consolation is that I know what's wrong and that alleviates some of the anxiety.

What I've got crystal clear though is that growing hole, the size of the ozone-hole, in my belly.

I cross the street to the TSB and sift through my wallet

for my ATM card. I come across Gabe's origami elephant. I smile to myself at its preciousness. I lodge it back into my wallet carefully and take out my ATM card, then slot it into the machine…

I go to punch in the four digits, but nothing happens because I can't remember. I have *never* forgotten my sacrosanct PIN number. It looks like the Alzheimer's is attacking the numbers department of my brain this week.

What I do remember is that I've got my numbers written on a little sticker on my card. How stupid is that? Very stupid. But imagine I write them down somewhere else and I can't remember where that somewhere else is. Reader, when you're dealing with Alzheimer's you've got to be ahead of yourself. Besides, I'm not going to lose my ATM card; forget it maybe, but not lose it.

I pull out the card, check the numbers, slot the card back in and thumb the buttons.

It looks like I've won the lottery when those twenties are spat out at me. I've never been so excited to see my own hard-earned cash. I'm starving! I swipe out the cash fast and roll head-long back across the street to the 24-hr (why a 24-hr in this town is beyond me, but I'm happy it is) fish 'n chip shop with my head down like a bull ready to gore somebody. 'Double fish 'n chip. I'm in a hurry, so if you wouldn't mind…'

The workers, two women and a man, creatures of the night, are leaning against their cookers with nothing to do but stare at yours truly. The blonde with the eyebrow piercing stares hard at me. I try to conceal my face below my trilby, but I must look ridiculous. She *knows* me. If she doesn't know me, then she knows there's something odd about me being here at this hour of the morning for supper. I just know it. She's seen me in the newspapers. I see her eyes flit at the door and the street beyond, looking for something roughly the size of an elephant waiting for that other fish 'n chip because why else would I order double if

I'm on my own?

'Could you close the door?'

'Hmm?'

'The door,' she repeats. 'There's a draught coming in. What can I get ya', love?'

I've forgotten what I came here for. I fiddle with my phone, as if checking my messages, but really trying to buy mili-seconds of time to avoid embarrassment. 'Um?'

The greasy-looking gent asks again in a foreign accent. 'What can we get you, sir?'

The other girl prompts, 'He asked for a double cod 'n chips.'

'Then why are you asking me if you know what my order is?' I'm real ratty. I don't want to be in any forgetting-situation more than necessary. 'Look, I'm in a rush.'

'Just checking,' Eye-Brow asks me. 'Take away?'

I nod. 'And a few bottles of water…' I repeat for good measure. 'A bottle of water…if you're going to ask me again.' I'm sick and tired of being humble. I decide that, from here on in, I'm going to stand up for myself and let's start with the double fish 'n chips. Who's on the run, after all?

She gazes at me momentarily, then swerves away on her heels and comes back at me with the water. I dig in my rucksack for my tablets and down them, draining off half the bottle while I'm at it. 'Another bottle of water. Give me five actually. I'll need them.'

The workers fire up the cooker especially for me. The woman tells me that it will be a few minutes and to take a seat. I hope I'm not waiting too long because I've an elephant to get back to.

Ten agonizing minutes later, they pass me my double cod 'n chips in a steamy, grease-stained brown paper bag. I pay and make for the door, but stall…

Where am I going?

I go outside, hoping the fresh air will jog my memory. I'm so lost right now that I don't even know if I live in this town, and why I am walking the streets at night. Maybe I live just up the street and decided I was hungry.

Without warning, the end of this tightrope I am walking materializes back into view ahead of me. I know where I am going once again and trot forward with my fish 'n chip supper. Walking back up that short-cut from the square, I fear that this thrill-ride is coming to a squealing stop, Reader. My condition is going to get one of us hurt or in trouble. I've had more black-outs this night than any other.

On my way up the street, I find a shop with an old woman, much older than yours truly, busying herself around the counter. What time is it?! It must be the middle of the night! I check my watch and my stomach does a flip when I see that it's just after 6 am. And sure enough, I look upwards and my lucky stars are beginning to fade and I see silver on the night-sky horizon. The sun will be up in no time and here I am doing a waltz with my double fish 'n chip. Oh, mercy. I've been here half the night – a stolen night, unfortunately Alzheimer's being my mistress. It has left me in a time-warp.

I scorn myself, 'You've got to get back to Sinbad…'

But I see the old lady sorting today's newspapers, fresh off the printing press. She's still living in a time when people picked up the newspaper first thing in the morning. She's not big on the internet, I take it. This is my only chance to see if there's any more news about our escapades and how close the police are to closing in. 'It'll just take a second,' I convince myself .

I step inside the establishment.

It's an old-timin' shop and is full of tubs and gallons of sweets and chocolates. I pick a newspaper off the pile still on the ground waiting to be shelved. 'Can I help you lift those?' I ask, ever the gentleman, despite impending circumstances.

'You'll get grease all over 'em.' The woman points to the greasy bag in my hand with her arthritis-gnarled finger, 'Stinking up the place while you're at it, son...' She still hasn't looked at me but head down on the job at hand. She's been doing the same for half a century.

'Sorry. I'll just get the newspaper and be on my way.' For a second there, as I approached the shop, I thought she might be a little senile, but she's sharp as Toledo steel...

They say never do the shopping while hungry. The crumb-ham behind the glass of the counter-freezer looks too good to pass up. Nowadays it's just soggy slices in a packet. I haven't seen ham like this since my honeymoon. I order a few slices of that too. I must be losing my edge. What am I *doing?* I need to get back before sunrise. I'm like a vampire, Reader.

The woman behind the counter cuts me a few slices with a meat-slicer of antique status just like its owner, only half as sharp. She may be ancient and balding, but she operates the meat-cutter like a professional. I flinch as her twisted fingers pass over the rotating blade.

'You open early...'

'Early to bed, early to rise, son.'

'Uh-huh.'

'I'm Isabella,' she says, cutting and grunting. 'but you can call me Bells. Everybody else does cos they hear me before they see me. They say I talk too much, but I think they don't talk enough.' She cackles at this and slurps from a cup of a steaming liquid which I presume is tea; she doesn't strike me as a coffee-drinker. 'And what's your name? I don't recognize you.' She looks at me with intent, watery, rheumatic sky-blue eyes for the first time.

'Gearóid,' I lie. Lies come easy these days. As matter of fact, I feel I'm living somebody else's life. I find it difficult to tell truth from fiction anymore, and I'm not sure if that's due to my Alzheimer's or not.

'A good Irish name!' Bells confirms. 'There was a time when people changed their Irish names to English names because of the times we lived in, but now people are going back to their roots and it's *cool*, as the young delinquents of this town say. Little bastards, every one of 'em,' repeating for emphasis: '*Bastards*.' She slaps the crumb-ham slices onto a sheet of paper and takes a feeble bite from a sandwich she had hidden behind the counter and slurps…*slurps*…slurps more tea. 'What brings you to Old Castle, son?'

'A goose. I'm chasing a wild goose, Bells.'

She nods. 'Not chasing an elephant, are you?'

'Huh?'

She titters which ends in a phlegmy wheeze and wipes her mouth. I'm beginning to have second thoughts about my crumb ham.

I freeze. 'Just a goose, Bells.'

She nods towards the stack of newspapers piled next to the magazines. 'Apparently, there's a hero in our midst. He wouldn't be the first, but he would be the first hero *not* from Old Castle. Our other heroes were born 'n bred right here in this town. Seems to be some kinda magnet for them. And remember Gerard, *Gearóid*, sorry, that heroes come in all sizes and colours.'

'Oh yeah?'

'Oh yeah,' she repeats. 'Not so long ago, Arthur Lawless, just down the street here, tried to set up his own circus. His plan fell flat on its arse, an outstanding flop, but didn't he give everybody else a lift in this town. Gave us hope, y'know, *hope*.' She waves her deformed fist a little. 'I've got this corner dedicated to his cause.'

I look at the bizarre mini-shrine of items on sale, custom-designed circus oddities.

'A little industry has built up around the spectacular flop, so who's the winner in the end? Arthur Lawless is mayor now.' She cackles again. 'He's got a very unusual

146

pet, but I'm not allowed to talk about that.' She zips her lips and drops the imaginary key somewhere down her front.

Don't worry, Reader, I won't be going to look for it.

'Willy Moone came before Lawless.'

'Is that right?' I check my watch. These names mean nothing to me right now, but I don't want to seem rude – call it my upbringing.

'He ran off with a gypsy.'

'Good for him...'

If looks could kill, Reader. 'Hmm. They had a daughter who spoke with the dead – then she went at it full-time before she went and topped herself, poor devil. Whatever floats yer boat...'

'Okay, so how much for the...'

'Before any of 'em was Jonny Rowe and his balloon.'

'His balloon?'

'He put us on the map. We all got a slice.' Bells chuckles to herself and gestures to the small stack of books for sale on the counter. 'Books have been written about the sons of Old Castle. Can't keep 'em on the shelves.'

'Good. Selling well.'

'No, I just can't keep 'em on the shelves, so I keep 'em on the counter here.'

On the book cover, I see a man floating overland, holding onto a red balloon. Maybe I should buy a copy. I'll have time to read it when they put me away, either in an old folks' home or prison.

Bells stares at me and grows thoughtful.

Before she speaks, I lose my cool, and split from the shop before things get any more personal, forgetting the crumb-ham, but paying for three king-size Snickers instead. This whole night-time trip is becoming more surreal by the minute.

I hear Sinbad before I see him. He's down by the stream. I have to look to find him, eventually following the intermittent clang of the bell to see him in the early-morning shadows.

It's true; unless you're looking for an elephant you won't find one.

The cold, silver light of dawn is beginning to creep in and I fear I've made a terrible mistake, Reader. Maybe you even saw it coming before I did. I've come too far in off the secluded briar and bush landscape. As the park lights up, I see that this is a town-park and the kind of place mothers take their kids for walks and young lovers go to get away.

'We're trapped.'

Sinbad eyes me.

'Are you thinking what I'm thinking? Yeah, exactly, now what?'

Sinbad sighs dolefully and lies down to rest, slower than usual.

'You're getting old like me, Sinbad. Don't worry, there's nothing we can do about it except enjoy the ride while we can. Maybe it's time to turn ourselves in, buddy. And speaking of enjoying the ride…'

I use Sinbad's front leg as a step-up, grab his left ear and pull myself onto his back. Once I find a suitable and comfortable perch, I lay my head back, tuck into my fish 'n chip, and open the newspaper and almost slide off my elephant when I open the centre-page spread…

Cahoots

The entire centre pages are dedicated to our exploits, Sinbad and I. The article covers our journey southwest from the capital. It even draws a time-line and highlights where our 'heroic efforts' took place with approximate times.

The three children on a farm in County Tipperary maintain that an elephant pulled the unnamed, drowning girl from a slurry-pit. The only solid evidence is a Talking Tom app which had recorded a voice believed to be that of ex-keeper Mick Munroe. However, police are having difficulty identifying the voice due to its helium nature. At first, the children were dismissed regarding their "tall elephant tale", until this newspaper broke the story that Dublin Zoo's most beloved elephant, Sinbad, had been 'misplaced'. Though the children, unnamed for legal reasons, maintain the elephant went by the name of Sammy Davis Junior. Things started falling into place when a woman, who we interviewed at her hospital bed after having a tree crash through her windscreen in Newport, County Tipperary, recalls how a super-strong individual named Sinbad saved her life. Again, actual sighting of the elephant was eluded. However, the individual who rang the emergency service on her behalf, does fit "ex-keeper" Mick Munroe's profile.

But the biggest article is about foiling a major house robbery. I'm surprised to see that the owner of the house is a politician who would like to publicly thank me for my efforts. He goes on to make a public appeal for my whereabouts.

Is this a scam? Politicians *do* lie with great ease. He's in cahoots with the police. He'll lull me into a false sense of security, as they say in the nature documentaries, then take my elephant away from me and hand me into the authorities.

I need to get out of here!

'Sinbad, c'mon, we're –'

Sinbad raises to a standing position without having me to finish '...outta here...'

I'm all gung-fucking-ho, but wait...'Eat your fish 'n chips in peace,' I order myself, 'because it might be your last meal for a while.'

I agree with the person speaking through me. Is it my conscience or are other forces at work? Or maybe I'm just lonely and the sound of my own voice is a comfort now at this late/early hour.

I'm just about licking my fingers when the bottom falls out of my existence...

Brush with the Law

I find myself sitting on an elephant's back in a park with a cold bag of fish and chips, having no idea how I got here…I slide off the elephant's back and wander away, oblivious to what I'd been doing seconds previous.

I must look lost because a woman going for an early-morning jog asks me if I'm okay.

I don't know if I'm okay…

'Where are you going?'

How embarrassing. 'I've forgotten.'

She asks, growing more wary, 'Where are you coming from?'

I shake my head. Everything has gone out of focus though my vision is twenty-twenty. I feel like I've drunk too much and that last beer sent me over the edge of oblivion. Images flit in and out of my mind's eye, and I couldn't say if an hour or a minute has passed…

'Do you have a car? How are you travelling?' She jogs on the spot as if the apocalypse will come if she stops.

I look at the ground, trying to retrace my steps. 'I'm sorry, I um, I just…' The whole thing is very disconcerting, I don't know where I am but feel as if I should know the place or as if I've seen it in a vivid dream.

'Come with me,' she says, making a decision there and then. 'I know what we can do.' She walks ahead a little and turns back to me. 'Don't worry. It's just up here around this corner.'

In a daze, I follow the jogger, vaguely aware that dawn is growing brighter and brighter. She leads me up a street adjacent to the park I think I've just come from. I pass a row of terraced houses on my right. The wall plaque reads: *Connolly's Terrace*. We walk through the forecourt of a closed-down petrol station.

Finally, she stops jogging; here comes the apocalypse.

'C'mon.'

'Here??'

'No, that's a closed petrol station. Here…'

I look at the building she wants me to go into. It's a police station.

'The police can help you.'

'Can they?'

I follow her inside and stand at the sliding-window in the hallway with the jogger, lost like that little eight year-old kid again. I see a young policeman speaking on his phone in the little office. He hasn't seen us. He laughs occasionally, and I guess there aren't many crimes tonight. The woman takes the initiative and taps on the glass. The policeman swivels around on his chair and fumbles with his phone. He hangs up on his personal call and comes to the window, slides it open, and greets us with a wide smile that is almost a creepy grin. Reader, just to clarify, I know everything that's going on in front of me, but future and past have turned to dust particles.

The woman speaks for me. 'Hi. I met this man down the street and I think he is amnesiac or, or something.'

'I hardly think that's a police matter?' scoffs the young man. 'I watch some telly when I can't sleep.'

'No, sorry. You don't understand. You're referring to insomnia. Um, this man cannot remember anything and um,' glancing at me, 'he looks sober.'

'Hello, my name is Derek,' says the policeman. 'What's your name?' He speaks loudly and slowly, as if I'm mentally disabled.

I shake my head.

'Would you mind showing me your wallet and we'll see if we can find a name there?'

'Okay.'

I take out my wallet and hand it over as innocently as a child would take sweets from a stranger.

We watch the policeman quickly sifting through the

contents of my wallet. He takes out a piece of folded paper which is, in fact, an origami elephant. He holds it up to me. 'Cute. Does this jog your memory?'

It means nothing to me right now; don't know how it got there.

'Hmm. I could never get the dragon right – always looked as if its wings were too small for its body,' he yells. 'You have no identification here. But I *can* reveal something…' he says with a glint in his eye.

'Yes?' asks the woman, with her head almost in over the counter.

'This man likes Snickers. He's got nothing but wrappers in here. But no name or address. Not even a bank card…'

The mention of a Snickers seems to fire up my failing memory and I realize, to my detriment, where I am…

Oh, mercy, Reader. I'm in the lion's den. The policeman has a known law-breaker standing in front of him – virtually turning himself in – and he doesn't know it. All he needs is to ID me and Bob's your uncle, say goodbye to your elephant, Mick. I *must* play along…

'He's a ghost,' laughs the policeman. 'He doesn't have one card on him that tells us who he is. Not even a dentist appointment card.'

Now, it's my turn to put on the best acting performance of my career to date – the *only* acting performance of my career to date.

Here we go…

'Eureka!' I rejoice, over-acting. 'It's all coming back to me. Now I know what I was doing.' I grab my wallet and its contents, apologize profusely to the jogger and the policeman, backing down the hallway. 'Sorry, I suffer bouts of insomnia.'

The policeman looks at the jogger with raised eyebrows that say: *told you so…*

I beat a hasty retreat from the police station, thanking everybody profusely for their help, and even bowing at one stage. 'But now I've got it all under control, thank you.' More bows, rictus smiles... I leave the building, snapping a quick selfie with the lit sign *Police Station* in the background, just to remember the moment I almost handed myself in.

But now, there's something bugging me, and it's not only the fact that I've been away far too long from Sinbad *plus* it's the morning! What's worrying me now, Reader, is that the yelling policeman had said that I had no identification, not even a card!

Frantically, I check my wallet. It's not there! My bank card isn't there! I left it in the goddamn ATM! '*Fucking moron!!*' Excuse my French, Reader. Who doesn't swear?

Torn between going back to Sinbad and retrieving my card, I decide Sinbad is more important right now. If he's seen, well, the four-tonne cat is out of the bag, but chances are that my card is still in the ATM because people generally sleep at night rather than withdraw money. Yet, I'm relying on that card for food. Then again, prison meals are free. What would *you* do, Reader?

Elephant versus Bank Card? Hmm...

The fact of the matter is that this whole adventure is going down the drain if the Indian elephant is spotted. It's all about the elephant.

I gallop back to the park under the orange glow of the streetlights...that have just blinked out. It is officially morning. I trot-walk all the way down to the end of the park, heaving myself over several gates and crossing a little bridge built over a stream. I'm making a habit of this. How many times in the last twelve hours have I taken this route? Too many is the answer and that's just during my lucid hours. Where have I been in my forgetfulness?

And there is Sinbad. I see him standing on the bank of the stream. He's drinking water and spraying himself in a shower while his sheep-bell rings. A low fog coats the dewy countryside as the sun comes up over the hills to the west. This, Reader, is the memory I will lock away. It's romantic and majestic. And just to back it up, I take a photo, so I will cherish it forever. At the same time, I'm thinking: thank God this area is so far down into the park; people tend to stay on the side nearer town. But it is only a matter of time before we are seen. I am betting Sinbad is seen first.

My elephant is okay for now, but forty years of friendship has told me that he's going to get bored soon and go wandering. I'm tempted to reassure him that I'm here, but maybe it's better to say nothing. I don't want to break his fun. I turn on my heels and head back the way I came, expecting a memory block any minute now so every second counts. It's a race against my own memory.

Five minutes later, I approach the TSB, praying that my card is still in the ATM slot... but it's empty.

Now what? Then I remember that I stuck a little white sticker on there with my – oh, Mercy! – PIN. What was I thinking, you're probably asking yourself, Reader. Well, I was thinking that I forget numbers a lot lately and actually forgetting my *card* never entered the equation. Stupid, yes. You don't need to tell me. Definitely ranks in the most stupid things I've ever done. I never expected to *lose* the card! I thought the chances were higher of me forgetting the numbers rather than losing my card, but I've now done both on this trip.

But it doesn't finish there, Reader.

I also included my name and phone number, should I ever lose it. Talk about a fucking moron. If Gloria was around these things wouldn't happen. If Gloria was around she'd kick my arse from here to Timbuktu and back again...

So, now I've got yet another predicament. All these predicaments, by the way, depend on the finder of my card. If it is found (was found) by a dishonest person, I can kiss my life-savings goodbye. If it's found by an honest person, then they'll probably turn it in to the police and then the shit-storm will begin to blow from the east. Will they ring the police? They will read my name on the bank card. They might try and turn me in for a reward if they realize whose card they have. If that other dishonest imaginary card-finder appears, then they could ring me and blackmail me…A kind of nice way of siphoning out my money because they have the PIN anyway. But horror of horrors!!! What if the finder is in cahoots with that politician who wants to personally (and publicly) thank me for stopping his house being robbed before turning me into the authorities!

Key word: cahoots.

What a dilemma, Reader…

I don't like the idea that some stranger has my number, but worse still, I don't have theirs. Am I being paranoid, Reader?

Filled with blind panic, I run back through the park to my old friend, Sinbad. I'm completely disregarding my elephant, and I feel guilty for it. I got him into this mess.

When I get to him, he's grazing on riverside grass. At least I'm keeping the elephant hidden.

'Come, Sinbad.' I give him half a Snickers to persuade him. He jogs along at my heels for more as we head back to the stands.

'Sinbad, I just need to sit down for a minute, then I will take us to a safer spot. I feel vulnerable here. We need to get out of here fast. I think I know a way…' I give him the other half of the chocolate bar, and he does that thing where he squints up his eyes. Have you ever seen an elephant smiling, Reader? 'Those hills over there,' pointing in a south-westerly direction, 'we should aim for those.'

I spark up a cigarette and suck it down to the butt in five heavy drags. That calms my nerves (yeah, I know, not great for my lungs). I feel relaxed, at one with the whole goddamn thing.

'I just need to close my eyes for fifteen minutes to mentally plan the next leg of our journey, Sinbad. That's all I ask – fifteen minutes.'

I am overtaken by an overwhelming desire to close my eyes as *everything* catches up with me, 'just fifteen minutes …'

When I open my eyes again, I have a new perspective on my dilemma…

Smell the Coffee Beans…

Having a new perspective on my dilemma is one way of putting it…

I wake to the sound of giggling kids. I don't want to open my eyes and would love just to live out the rest of my days behind these closed eyelid shutters.

The kids laugh harder this time, obviously trying to get me to react. I give in and open my eyes to see seven or eight children looking down on me from the Heavens, but they're no angels. Then I hear deeper voices out of my line of view.

Then claps…and cheers…

And, oh fuck, what have I done?

I get to my feet to see a few hundred people looking – *staring* – at me from the stands to my right, cheering and screaming. I'm not sure whether to run or salute. But I quickly come to the conclusion that they're not looking at me but the two local football teams and Sinbad – *Sinbad, my elephant!* – between them, playing football!

Oh…Mercy!! I've overslept, haven't I, Reader? My capers have finally caught up with me and in what spectacular fashion. I couldn't have picked a better spot to sleep: in a football field in front of a football stand. I somehow wandered from the stands to the centre of what is apparently a football pitch during my hours of sleep, which were intended to be 15 minutes shut-eye to get my thoughts straight.

The crowd is eating it up, capturing it all on their phone cameras and whatever else they can find to freeze the moment.

It's over… is all I can think as the crowd chants, over and over again:

'Sinbad! Sinbad! Sinbad!'

'Yep, it is definitely over,' I say to myself with a smile

on my face, watching Sinbad like a little baby elephant calf.

I can see the delight in his face, slapping the ball ahead of him with his trunk and front legs while the players dance around him. It's a sight for sore eyes, Reader. This is so strange. I've spent the last few nights avoiding people and now here I am in the middle of a football pitch *during* a football game. But where are the police? Am I dreaming? A part of me screams YES, but another part of me screams NO. I'm not sure which I prefer, Reader. I want our adventure to go on forever, but at the same time, I want it to end. I'm so, so tired and my condition is worsening, seemingly by the hour. Time to wake up and smell the coffee beans...

Before I know what's happening, I'm being talked into joining the St. Patrick's Day parade in Old Castle that will begin in an hour from now – by the kids of Old Castle, they're doing the talking.

'Pleeease!' pleads a little girl. 'We've never had an elephant before – a donkey, but not an elephant!'

'Yeah,' says a boy, and repeats exactly what the little girl had said: *'Pleeease...'*

'By the way,' says the girl, 'is it Sammy Davis Junior or Sinbad?'

Still in shock, I just manage, 'Uh, Sinbad...'

Then their folks get in on the act and ask me to be part of their parade. 'Please,' I quieten down the football/Sinbad fans. 'We're honoured, but what you're suggesting is crazy. I knew this adventure would have to come to an end soon, but...'

A steady clap begins...growing into a full-blown applause. 'Hero! Hero! Hero!'

Goosebumps shiver my arms and legs, and I begin to cry. I cry because it's all over, but I also shed a tear for what I have come to represent to these people. I couldn't have ever dreamt this would be the outcome of my crazy idea to steal an elephant and walk cross-country by night, guided by the stars. 'I didn't think it would end like this.' I wipe the tears from my cheeks and the same little girl gives me a paper tissue that resembles a golf ball and just as hard, probably having gone through the washing-machine.

I chuckle and so do the others. 'In case you haven't noticed, I'm wanted by the police for stealing an elephant.'

'We would've done the same!' Somebody shouts back, followed by a sea of nodding heads.

'There will be police all over town,' I tell them. 'How do you expect an elephant to take part in a parade and not be seen? Sinbad and I are on the run…The police will put me behind bars and Sinbad will be exiled to spend a life behind bars too, but with a sadist as an excuse for a zoo-keeper. Please, *please*, help me hide…'

'You and Sinbad are heroes!' yells a girl.

A man comes forward from the crowd. 'It's true. You two are like Batman and, um, what's the other…'

'Robin…' prompts another fan.

'You two are legend! Travelling by night and saving people or solving crimes as you go. What can the *police* do?? The people love you!'

If only Smiler was here to see this. 'Look, I would love to take part in your parade, but the police will contact the zoo and the zoo will be down from Dublin in three hours with a lorry and that will be the last I will see of my elephant. Sinbad and I have worked side by side for four decades. I was recently let go from my position due to an illness that I have – fair enough, I understand that. I shouldn't have kept it a secret and that led to problems. But my illness was used as an excuse to get me out for an abusive zoo-keeper who was only hired because he's a nephew of the hiring 'n firing woman in the HR department. The only animal experience he has was that he owned a couple of guinea-pigs when he was eight years old – George and Mildred I think he called them.'

Big laughs from the crowd.

'I suffer from Alzheimer's.'

I feel like it's my first night at an AA meeting with all the home-truths. 'I've been hiding it for as long as I could because I didn't want to lose my job. I kept it a secret longer than I should've and mistakes were made. I take full responsibility for what happened, but I was left with no option. I couldn't stand by and watch my dear friend being abused.'

This gets a few sorry and concerned smiles, but one woman laughs out of turn.

'I might not remember any of this tomorrow. This is why I've taken my elephant. I want something to remember. I've already forgotten what my recently-deceased wife looks like. What I have is a vague photo-slide memory, but not herself at home. I can't hear her voice anymore.' I flash a consolatory smile but aware that I'm beginning to fall back on my dead-wife-take-pity-on-me excuse. I *refuse* to let that happen, Reader. 'We didn't know where this trip would take us – certainly not to a football field full of football fans.'

Somebody shouts back. 'We are your fans!'

'Now you said it!' another yells back.

'Please, take part in the parade. Think Elephant Pride instead of Gay Pride!'

Another round of raucous laughter.

'Be proud of who you are!'

Another warming cheer for me and I redden up.

I have to admit that I'm considering joining the parade. It's all over now anyway. The amusement ride has come to a stop; time to undo my seatbelt. Old Castle is the end of the line for me, as the saying goes, so why not go out on a high note, Reader? 'Okay, we'll do it!'

'The parade is unadulterated shit every year,' squawks a skin-head teenager, 'but this is going to be the best year yet!'

I approach my elephant.

A little girl comes up to me. Her father, who is holding her hand, spurs her on. Shyly, she hands me a Snickers. 'We read that he likes Snickers.'

Her little angelic face turns me to putty. 'You read right.' I peel the wrapper and give the chocolate bar to the girl. 'Give it to him yourself. He won't bite. He hardly has any teeth left.'

'Can I give half to my sister? I bet she'd love to feed Sinbad, too.'

The girl points to a little blonde girl standing next to us. I break the bar of chocolate and hand half to her. 'And what's your name?'

'Chloe,' she tells me in her cute, shy little way.

Squeamishly, the oldest sister hands up the chocolate bar to Sinbad and he takes it with gentlemanly grace, then curls it upwards into his mouth...

'What's your name?'

'Maia.'

'Maia, watch his ears,' I tell her, 'he'll flap them to say thanks.'

And on cue, Sinbad flaps his ears to another round of applause. The little girl jumps up and down in sheer delight.

Then the little sister takes her turn to feed my elephant, equally astounded as her sister.

I know Maia and Chloe will remember this for the rest of their lives, just as the other kids who have met Sinbad along the way.

I turn to the crowd. 'Gimme a leg up somebody. No wait...' I take my Canon from my backpack and surprise everybody by getting them to stand in around me for one last selfie. 'I can't forget this...'

Snap...

Box of Matches

I put my camera back in my backpack and five volunteers help me climb onto Sinbad's back. I sit in behind his ears like an Indian mahout. We move off, following the crowd walking ahead of us. The football game continues with no supporters, so that game falls apart and the teams join our cause in their shorts and football jerseys. This whole thing has become as absurd as my kidnapping of the elephant. If it were a book, I'd say *anything* is possible in fiction.

Sinbad and I are led down through the park towards the town square where the Saint Patrick's Day parade is doing a lap of the town. Just a few hours ago, I was here, *several* times, and the place was a ghost town. People line the streets and when they see us joining the parade there is a moment of suspended disbelief before a huge cheer erupts. People go wild. Kids and parents alike wave their green, white, and gold flags at us.

We join the parade, slipping in behind a Smurfs float. The Smurfs – who had been the star of the show – dance harder to compete with the old man and his elephant.

Then I see the police… 'This is it, Sinbad.'

I can see them beginning to group and come in my direction. This is what I've been waiting for, Reader. This is the *fucking* showdown that I've really wanted since I stole Sinbad on that fateful night. I see what they're at. I want *justice*. They're going to try to steer me away without stopping the parade; discreetly remove the elephant from the room.

'Keep going, Sinbad…' I kick him on with my heels, almost running us into the Smurfs and staying right up behind them; never thought I'd get so close to a Smurf's ass. The police try to intervene, but I keep Sinbad lodged to the Smurfs. One of the barriers lining the street is lifted up ahead and a squad car sneakily edges into the parade and tries to prize itself between my elephant's trunk and the Smurfs. The onlookers suddenly see what's trying to happen, flags fall and a hush descends behind the blaring parade music...

Suddenly, a voice booms around the town square. 'Mick Munroe...'

I turn to my right to see a man in a suit standing on an empty trailer-float parked up in front of the castle that dominates Old Castle's square.

'Please, calm down,' the man pleads, meanwhile the police close in. 'I am indebted to you and your elephant...and the list of people who want to thank you is growing... We are all indebted to you, Mick. You are some kind of angelic saviour who has come in the night. Please, don't run anymore. We would like to take care of you and help with your condition that *everybody* is aware of because people aren't watching *Eastenders* anymore; they're tuning into the news to get the latest round of updates on your adventures. You and your elephant are larger than life, and we just want to repay our debt... My name is Arthur Lawless. I am the mayor of Old Castle. I want to make you an honorary citizen of our little town.'

Where have I heard that name before? Lawless?

For a brief hallucinatory moment, I swear on my heart and soul that I see a monkey standing side-stage, holding hands with two girls. But Sinbad's on default mode and I can't stop him...

People lining the streets begin to gravitate towards the squad-car to see what's going to happen next...

A plain-clothes policeman in his late fifties steps out of the car and waves his hands at the people to quieten them. 'The mayor can give you anything he wants, the key to the town even, but Mick is wanted by law for theft of an elephant. I'm the law-man and I'm taking him in and confiscating the elephant. After that, the mayor can feed you on lollipops for all I care. I've got a job to do...'

Chaos is what happens next…

St Patrick's Day parade manifests into an all-out craze-fest. People scream and shout, shamrocks fly through the air. People put their lives at risk by jumping in front of the police car and pull at the windshield wipers. I can't hear what's going on, but they're defending me. The police are overcome and scramble back into their vehicle. People surround the car and blind the police inside with their waving flags. The music suddenly stops, the Smurfs get really irate now and blankly refuse to do anymore samba or truffle-shuffles. People shout and scream at the police that Sinbad and I are "legends and heroes" and we should be "left alone and be free!"

I think about disappearing up the same alley we had appeared from just a few minutes previous. But there are people *everywhere* and I'll only end up killing one of them, rather Sinbad will, but it's the driver that's guilty, not the car. It's like being stuck in rush-hour traffic. I have no choice but to sweat it out and get around to the other side of the square before I can take one of the streets…before I'm caught by the authorities. But what's the point of running now anyway?

Meanwhile, the parade has turned into an ugly protest and people have forgotten the cause of their protest and now protest for every wrong-doing they've ever suffered in their lives. It seems as if this town has been on the brink of an outcry and all it needed was the match to set it alight. I'm the box of matches, Reader.

Blaring music comes back into life to calm or hide the situation. Police merge from left and right and try to slow my elephant, but they're not that stupid, so back off. The parade keeps moving ahead despite chaos. The Smurfs are not sure whether to dance or scream, and I can see the worry on their blue faces.

Finally, we do another slow-mo lap of the square before a sea of people in front of me divide and I make a break for it.

'*Run* like you've never run before, Sinbad!'

I dig my heels into his shoulders. And he *does* run, Reader...and I pay the price, trying to hold onto anything I can find a grip on, like his ears, for example. I slip off his left side and dangle from his ear and he hardly seems to notice as he trundles along, full steam ahead, trunk pointing southwest.

A group (possibly Old Castle vigilantes) escort me out of town. Behind me, I hear the clash of riots. I recall old Bells telling me something about other individuals who have lifted Old Castle's spirits. I didn't mean to raise their spirits this high. What has brought me to Old Castle? Luck? Sinbad? Is Old Castle a magnet for dreamers?

Should I have just let the police take over? I've had a good run. But now that I see a tiny chance of escaping from the police, I feel that this isn't over yet...

We bail on Old Castle, but not ten minutes out of town, at a cross-roads in the middle of nowhere, I see the outline of a woman waving to me. She is shimmering in the mid-day sun bouncing off the tarmac.

For a second, I think it's my Glow welcoming me to a place where we will never be found again...under the apple-tree in the back yard.

The Mirage

'Mick! This way!'

She's calling me. Do I know her? Am I currently going through one of my amnesiac bouts? Should I know her? She is nothing but a mirage…

She waves and calls again, 'Mick Munroe, down here…' in scolding tones as if she were my mother and I'd just done something out of line. As I approach, I see that she's pointing down a country lane, and I have no choice but to take her advice because all I see beyond her is a mile-stretch of nothing but road.

I steer Sinbad left into the lane (or rather Sinbad takes the initiative and does it by himself). Police sirens come up behind me. We pull in behind a bush of whitethorn and blend with the colours. The squad cars, three in all (didn't think I was so important), pull up at the gate I just came through. I vaguely hear the short conversation over my thumping heart:

'Have you seen him?'

'Who?' asks the woman – the mirage – with award-winning conviction.

'You know who, Sarah,' answers the plain-clothes, obviously knowing the woman.

'I'm just waiting here for my son. We're going to eat out today on account of it being Paddy's Day. We have booked a table at the –'

'You can tell me all about it once I catch up with Elephant Man…'

I hear a car-door slam shut and the rev of engines…and the cars are gone.

A wave of relief washes over me, and I almost slide off my elephant for the second or third time today.

The woman appears and smiles up at me, shielding her eyes from the sun.

167

I thank her.

'There's nothin' as borin' as listening to an old woman jabbin' on about her lunch. I'm Sarah, by the way.'

'Yeah, I heard. I'm…well, you know who I am.' I tell her anyway, 'Mick Munroe.'

She laughs. 'I *know*. It's written here.' She holds up something and, for a moment, I've no idea what she's getting at.

'I found your bank card. Well, my son found it actually. He works nights at the water-bottlin' plant here in town and went to take some cash out, as one does.'

I can't believe what I'm hearing. 'What are the chances?' is all I manage to say.

The mirage called Sarah goes on. 'I tried to ring, but your phone was off. I guess we were meant to meet anyway.'

'Dead battery. I don't have a charger. It's one of those old brick Nokias and I wouldn't charge it for days on end at home. Time caught up with it. Do you have a charger?' I laugh.

'You don't need one now.' She dismisses this as if everything in the world is going to be okay from today onwards – or else the world is going to end from today onwards, or maybe she has a new way of charging phones without chargers. Her tone of voice could be read as: *you won't need it where you're going.* Sarah nods over her shoulder. 'I live down at the bottom of the lane. I've got a whole ghost farm down there.'

I'm a little taken aback by this comment as I've also lived in a ghost house since my Glow passed. 'You're farming ghosts? Is there much money in that these days?'

She titters; maybe it's a charity-giggle for the senile old man on the elephant. I can't help feel that I've met this mirage somewhere before on another lonely landscape. 'No,' she replies, 'though there's probably more money in it than cattle. My husband passed away last year and I decided to sell up the animals and stay on the farm because of memories more than anythin' else.'

'I understand that, though I'm losing mine.'

Sarah nods. She knows already. 'I can't see myself livin' anywhere else. It's a lot of work, but I'm not afraid of hard work, and I've got five grown sons to juggle the chores. So why should I move to an old folks' home?' She glances over her shoulder. 'I'm just makin' lunch and I'd be honoured if you and Sinbad would stay for somethin' to eat. I've always wanted to adopt an elephant, but never thought I'd actually really adopt an elephant. I send money every year to the baby elephants orphaned to the ivory trade.'

Sarah is a Pandora's Box; she's an admirable woman with admirable intentions, but my stomach is rumbling since hearing the 'lunch' word. 'I heard you mention that you're going out for lunch…'

'I couldn't think of anythin' else to say.'

I smile.

'There's more than enough room for your elephant and yourself. The police won't bother you down here. Nobody bothers an old widow livin' down a country lane. I've been followin' your plight on the telly and newspapers. I think it's a disgrace how they have treated you – like a fugitive. But the normal Joe Soap on the street thinks you're a breath of fresh air.'

'Don't blame the authorities; they're just doing their job…and I *did* commit a crime.'

'Still, you've more than made up for it in my book. You saved a child's life for starters…'

I give her the old cliché: 'Anybody would've done the same.'

Sarah leads us down the country lane. The weather is sweltering. In the hazy distance, I see the barn-top quivering in the heat-waves.

I can't shake the feeling that I'm coming home, Reader.

Epilogue of Sorts

Where do Elephants go to Die?

I stay on at Sarah's place after lunch – *months* after lunch.

Sometimes, I think that I might have found a new soul-mate, but then Sarah lets me down by saying or doing something my Glow would never say or do, but Sarah *does* come close. But isn't that just the spice of life? Everybody is different. Sarah *is* a mirage after all; an oasis in this arid, amnesiac, desert mindscape. I fear if I get too close she, too, will turn to dust. So I keep my distance and admire her from it.

On mild days, Sarah and I sit out on deckchairs in the yard, watching Sinbad graze and wander at his leisure in the five-acre paddock that stretches out at the back of the farmhouse. The place is surrounded by apple-trees (funnily enough) and we eat apple tart and drink home-made apple cider that gives one *hell* of a fermenting kick. Oh, mercy. Sarah isn't afraid to sip from a glass of her rocket fuel. She informs me that it's the only "waywardness" she engages in. We sit and talk until late evening. Sarah tells me that she used to be a nurse and has some experience with Alzheimer's and dementia patients. We let on all is normal, even when I don't know where I am or what I'm doing, which will account for the gaps in this journal which I started last March. It is now September, Sarah tells me, the exact date escapes both of us. Sarah shows me various photographs of elephants in far off countries that she has adopted. Having a real elephant in her home is the next logical step, she reckons. We laugh at that, too. Sarah, the mirage, is a breath of fresh air.

We don't get any visitors except her five sons that have been sworn to secrecy that they are hiding an elephant and its keeper. Now and again, there is panic when the post-van comes bouncing down the lane. That's when I go hide. Sinbad's paddock cannot be seen from the front of the house. I often think about the mayor's offer of freedom in Old Castle, but I think I've got it right here on the outskirts of town. It's a catch-22, Reader. If I reveal myself to the mayor, I also reveal myself to the authorities. I'm a fugitive of my time, as somebody once said.

As the weeks pass, my elephant and I become the stuff of legend. How we came in the night, put the world to rights, and vanished. And vanish I did, Reader. I told Smiler where I was and that I have everything that I need. He's looking after the house, not that there's much to look after. I paid off my mortgage a few years back. I'll go back when the time's right or I just might sell up and move in with Sarah full-time. She has hinted at the idea. I'm *also* okay for clothes. It's a little macabre, Reader, but I wear a dead man's clothes. You see, Sarah never had the heart to throw out her husband's belongings. And it just happens that we are the same size. And, being a miser, suits me down to the ground. My only complaint is the canary-yellow trousers which *doesn't* suit me. I put it on for kicks every now and again (my lucid days) and that gives Sarah a good laugh. She looks thirty years younger when she smiles and a twenty year-old when she giggles. She tells me that this *is* therapy for her – seeing another man wear her deceased husband's clothes.

'Whatever floats your boat.'

But, Reader, I have some sad news to report. I thought I'd get the happy stuff out of the way first… It's why I'm here writing this in the first place. I'm not afraid to tell you that the ink smudges here on this page are where my tears fall.

This morning, Sinbad went missing. Sarah and I searched for him in all his usual haunts, but to no avail, so Sarah took the four-by-four and went cross-country. Ten minutes later, she drove back into the yard and I knew. I just knew… I sat into the jeep without a word and she took us downhill to the furthest corner of the paddock that lay in a blind spot, away from the farm and everything else.

Under an enormous apple tree, the biggest I've ever seen, was Sinbad, stretched out. It's true: elephants do go away to die. I cannot help but think that I am going in the same way.

We (Sarah, her five sons, me, and a JCB digger) have buried Sinbad in that same hidden, tranquil corner. I cannot think of a nicer place for him. It was almost as hard as putting Gloria in the ground, but at least I get to bury Sinbad in Sarah's backyard *and* under an apple tree. What are the chances? As a mark of respect, Sarah hung his tail-bell from the roof of the farmhouse porch.

Each day now is the first day for me because I cannot remember yesterday. I've lost count of everything and if Sarah told me that we were husband and wife, I would believe her. She shows me photographs of the same man over and over again with a variety of people and places behind him in the background. Apparently, that man is me.

Just yesterday, I was sitting out in the backyard when a sudden gust of wind got up and blew through the wind-chime. Only there was something vaguely familiar about the jingle-jangle of that wind-chime. I knew it meant something the moment I heard it and could *almost* remember what.

Sarah tends to me every day and she says that it's good to feel "wanted" again. I cannot say I share her enthusiasm. I never thought I'd find so much so late. I truly believe Sinbad led me to Sarah. His memory lives on in these pages, Reader, as does mine.

I won. I am a human with resources.

The End

Toledo, Copenhagen, Edinburgh.

September, 2015.

Jonathan's Novels:

Balloon Animals 2012

Living Dead Lovers 2013

The Nobody Show 2014

Hide the Elephant 2015

Hearts Anonymous 2016

Lighthouse Jive Coming Soon!

Jonathan can be found here:

Goodreads @
https://www.goodreads.com/author/show/6546212.Jonatha
n_Dunne

Blog @ http://jonathanwdunne.wordpress.com/

Twitter @ WriterJDunne

38702869R00112

Made in the USA
San Bernardino, CA
11 September 2016